**"I'm not ready for this."
His voice caught on the last word
as his fingers grasped the railing.**

Kyra clasped Michael's arm, wishing she'd been able
to prevent Amy from running away this morning at
the Pattersons'. But if Amy had stopped, the killer
would have shot her in the back. "Remember, I'm
here for you. We'll find your sister, and I'll make sure
she's safe."

He pried loose his grip from the railing and peered
toward her. "I appreciate your help. I've never had
something like this happen to me."

She was all too familiar with a person agonizing
over the disappearance of a loved one. "Most people
thankfully don't."

"Flamingo Cay is a small town. Things like this don't
happen here."

"They do now."

Books by Margaret Daley

MARGARET DALEY

feels she has been blessed. She has been married more than thirty years to her husband, Mike, whom she met in college. He is a terrific support and her best friend. They have one son, Shaun. Margaret has been writing for many years and loves to tell a story. When she was a little girl, she would play with her dolls and make up stories about their lives. Now she writes these stories down. She especially enjoys weaving stories about families and how faith in God can sustain a person when things get tough. When she isn't writing, she is fortunate to be a teacher for students with special needs. Margaret has taught for more than twenty years and loves working with her students. She has also been a Special Olympics coach and has participated in many sports with her students.

HIDDEN IN THE EVERGLADES

Margaret Daley

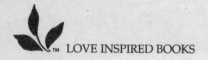

LOVE INSPIRED BOOKS

Recycling programs for this product may not exist in your area.

ISBN-13: 978-0-373-67478-7

HIDDEN IN THE EVERGLADES

Copyright © 2011 by Margaret Daley

www.LoveInspiredBooks.com

Printed in U.S.A.

Casting all your care upon Him,
for He careth for you.
—1 *Peter* 5:7

To Jan, who helped me brainstorm this book—
thank you

ONE

A wave broke and rolled across the white sandy beach, the warm water bubbling around Kyra Morgan's feet before receding back into the Gulf of Mexico. The sun peeked over the tops of the palm trees behind her, flooding the day with light. Her favorite time, at dawn when all was still right with the world. Before her day began.

The screech of a seagull pierced the tranquillity. A momentary disturbance until everything went back to a calmness that she'd needed after spending six straight years establishing Guardians, Inc. into a premier international company of female bodyguards. Drawing in a soothing breath, she relished the scent of the sea mingling with the sweet fragrance of the flowers her dad had planted right before his death a few years ago.

This was her time to rest and relax. One week in Flamingo Cay, Florida, where she'd grown up. One week of no work. No emergencies. No—

A click and muffled pop invaded her tranquillity.

Sounds she'd heard as a police officer.

She pivoted, her survival instinct kicking into play as she raced to her beach bag a few yards away. When she reached it, she plunged her hand inside and grasped the handle of her Glock while panning the house next door where the sound of a gun with a silencer going off had come from.

Another pop invaded the early-morning quiet. She started moving toward the noise. Every sense locked on finding the source of the danger.

Suddenly a young man burst out of the hibiscus hedge edging the neighbor's property, staggering toward her, his face clenched in pain. He clutched his stomach, blood pouring out between his fingers. Stopping, he fell to his knees, a plea in his eyes as they homed in on Kyra.

"Help us."

Us? Kyra glanced around as she covered the short distance to the young man. He collapsed to the sand, his eyes wide-open, giving her the dead man's stare she'd seen countless times as a homicide detective. She felt for his pulse and found none.

She pulled her cell from her shorts pocket and dialed 911. "Shots have been fired at 523 Pelican Lane. One man down—dead."

Another shot, coming from inside the house, sent a spurt of adrenaline through her veins. "Hurry." She disconnected, stuffed her phone into her pocket and ran toward the neighbor's back deck—the sliding glass door was partially open. The house was up for sale. She'd noticed the sign out front when she'd arrived yesterday evening. She hadn't thought anyone was living there.

Every nerve tingled with the threat of danger, but she couldn't get the young man's plea out of her mind. *Help us.* Who else was in trouble?

As she neared the back that faced the water, she slowed, scanning the overgrown yard. The place had a vacant look to it, with no furniture on the deck. She ascended the stairs and crept toward the sliding glass door. Through it she looked inside. Totally empty.

When she stepped over the threshold into the living room, a large expanse of taupe-colored tiles, her heartbeat accelerated. She paused and listened for any noise that indicated where the killer was.

Silence.

Another pop echoed through the vacant house, coming from the hallway that led to the bedrooms. A scream cleaved the air. The sound of pounding footsteps racing down the corridor toward Kyra propelled her into action. She flattened herself against the wall, her gun up, her total concentration on the opening. Heart hammering against her rib cage, she waited.

A teenage girl burst out of the hall and darted across the room, blood on her hands and shirt, her features chiseled in fear. She glimpsed Kyra out of the corner of her eye and gasped, momentarily slowing. Their gazes connected for a few seconds. Kyra put her forefinger to her lips to indicate she keep quiet.

The intrusion of a deep gravelly voice saying, "You can't get away from me," leached the rest of the color from the teen's face. Her eyes grew huge. She sped toward the exit.

Kyra focused on the entrance into the living room while the racing footsteps of the girl resonated through the air. From the hallway a shot sounded, shattering the glass in the door. She glanced toward the girl to see her disappear down the stairs and into the backyard.

Any second she expected to see the killer burst into the living room to hunt down the teen and finish her off. Kyra stiffened, every muscle primed for action.

Five heartbeats later she knew something was wrong. She inched closer to the edge of the wall to peer into the corridor. The thundering in her head pulsated through her mind, sending out an alarm. One, two deep breaths and she swiveled out into the entrance, her Glock pointing toward the bedrooms. Emptiness taunted her.

Followed by a sliver of fear.

Had the killer sensed she was there waiting for him to appear? Did the girl's gasp alert him?

Maybe. Was he now lying in wait for her somewhere down this hall? Or did he flee out another way and was doubling around the house to go after the girl?

Each possibility only reinforced the peril. Kyra eased down the hall, approaching each room with caution. After a visual check from the doorway, she continued her search until she reached the last bedroom, its entrance wide-open. The silence lured her forward, at the same time cautioning her against the action.

The memory of the fright on the teen's face propelled her toward the room. The girl was no match for a killer. Swinging into the bedroom, every sense homed outward, she scanned the area. A young man lay face up, his eyes closed, his chest barely rising and falling. Blood pooled on the tile floor by him, in front of an open sliding glass door, as a soft breeze blew the curtains.

Had the killer already escaped? Or was he in the bathroom or closet? She slunk along the wall to the first door and threw it wide. After inspecting the empty closet, she quickly moved on. At the bathroom, the door was ajar, and she nudged it farther open. As soon as she assessed no threat, she hurried to the man on the floor to see if there was anything she could do.

Tattoos covering both arms and an elaborate black dagger inked on his neck, the victim, probably between eighteen and twenty-two, wore blue jeans, the bottoms encrusted with wet mud, and a snow-white T-shirt, now saturated with blood from multiple shots to his gut. In her line of work she'd seen lethal wounds. This was one of them.

She placed another call to 911 to let them know a person was critically injured in the bedroom of the vacant house and the shooter had fled the scene possibly pursuing a potential witness. As she hung up, a flash caught her attention out of the corner of her eye. Leaping to her feet, she saw a man dressed in camouflage plunge into the thick underbrush on the right side of the house—into the thicket that led to the swamp nearby.

Was he going after the girl to finish her off?

Kyra couldn't let that happen. She'd done all she could for the young man, but maybe she could protect the teenage girl from getting killed, too.

She rushed out onto the small deck at the side of the house and scoured the area for any sign of an accomplice or the witness, then followed the assailant into the tangle of vegetation.

Dr. Michael Hunt scrubbed his hands down his face, trying to keep awake after pulling an all-nighter with a patient, a mother who finally delivered her baby boy at 5:13 a.m. this morning. Pouring his third mug of coffee, he wandered toward his bedroom to change, so he could turn around and go back to the clinic for today's appointments. At least his partner would be back from vacation to help take some of the load off.

The blare of a siren halted Michael's progress. He glanced toward the front of his house. The sound grew closer. Curiosity led him toward the entryway. He opened his door as two police cars passed his home on Pelican Lane and came to a stop five houses down from his place.

The old Patterson house? Was someone hurt? No one lived there. Hadn't for the past six months, according to his kid sister, Amy.

He heard the click of the back door and swiveled around, catching a glimpse of his youngest sister hurrying down the hallway. What was Amy doing up so early? She wasn't a morning person. He started forward to find out where she'd been when the shrill ring of his phone sliced through the silence.

Not far from the table in the entryway where it sat, he snatched up the receiver. "Hello."

"Dr. Hunt, this is Officer Wilson with Flamingo Cay Police. A man is injured at the Pattersons' place. He was shot. An ambulance won't get here for at least fifteen more minutes from Clear Springs. Since you only live—"

"I'll be there." Michael grabbed his black bag from a chair nearby and headed out the front door.

The urgency in the officer's voice prodded him

to quicken his pace. As he neared the vacant house, Levi Wilson came around from the side, a frown on his face.

He waved Michael toward him. "There's a dead man on the beach, but there's one in the bedroom alive. Barely."

"Shot where?"

"In the gut."

Michael rushed up the steps to the small deck on the side of the house. Just inside the sliding glass door lay a young man, faceup. He'd seen his fair share of fatal gunshot wounds. This one looked bad.

Michael knelt on the tile floor next to the injured young man who moaned, fixing his eyes on Michael. The young man's eyes fluttered right before his head lolled to the side and the breath went out of him.

In seconds, Kyra plunged into the wooded area and found herself ankle-deep in muddy water, a tangle of green vegetation hemming her in. Up ahead, she spotted movement and pressed ahead, branches clawing at her. Sweat coated her face. The realization that she didn't know which way the young girl had gone hastened her pace, even though the soggy ground weighed each step down. She couldn't let the killer add another victim to his list.

As she progressed, she spied the trampled bushes and vines where the assailant had run through. Then suddenly she came out onto a path with boot prints, about size eleven, which headed toward the canal. If she could remember correctly, the old pier people in the neighborhood used was in that direction—at least it had when she'd been growing up in Flamingo Cay.

Quickening her pace, she kept combing the area for any sign the killer had deviated from the trail. In the background she heard sirens coming closer but decided to keep going after the assailant. Deep into the green jungle of plants, her old fear began to encroach in her mind, robbing her of her full concentration. She nearly tripped over a half-buried log, managing at the last second to steady herself.

A muzzled pop sounded, followed immediately by a bullet whistling by her ear. She ducked behind a cypress not far from the path. With the loud beating of her heart vying with the drone of the insects, she peeked around the tree. Another pop echoed through the swamp. Splinters of bark flew off the cypress. She waited a minute, inching toward the other side of the large tree. Aiming high in case the girl was nearby, Kyra squeezed off several shots.

The noise of a motor revving came from the canal. Kyra peered in that direction. Through the foliage she saw a motorboat pull away. She hurried toward the old pier about twenty yards away. By the time she got to the bank of the water, the craft had disappeared around a bend going south.

Breathing hard, she bent over and tried to fill her lungs with oxygen. From behind her sloshing footsteps announced she had company. She straightened, bringing her gun up, and whirled to face any new threat.

TWO

Kyra lowered her Glock when she saw Gabe Stanford, the Flamingo Cay police chief, and another officer hurrying down the path toward her. For the first time since she'd heard the muffled noise of the first gunshot she relaxed her tense muscles, rolling her head to work the aches out of her neck and shoulders.

Gabe stopped in front of her, a little out of breath. "This isn't the way I envisioned us meeting when your aunt told me you were finally coming home for a visit."

Smiling at the man who had been her inspiration to become a law-enforcement officer, she went to him and gave him a hug. "Me neither. I came back for my first vacation in six years and got caught up in a murder."

Gabe frowned, peered back at the officer and said, "I've got this, Connors. You can go back and help Wilson."

The large thirtysomething man nodded and retraced his steps toward Pelican Lane.

"What happened here? I was checking the yard by the swamp and heard gunshots." Gabe glanced down at the Glock.

"I returned the killer's fire. He ran out of the Pattersons', and I went after him. He shot twice at me then got into a motorboat and went that way." Kyra pointed to the south.

"Did you get a good look at him?" He holstered his gun.

"No. He was too far away and his head was turned from me. He was wearing camouflage pants and shirt, boots and a ball cap, pulled down low on his forehead. He was about six feet, slender build. That's all I got. Sorry." As a police officer for twelve years before founding Guardians, Inc., she knew the importance of a detailed and correct description of an assailant.

"It's better than a lot I've gotten. Did you see the man kill either victim back at the Pattersons'?"

She shook her head. "I did see him shoot at a girl who fled the scene. I don't think he hit her. I thought he might be going after her so I took off after him."

"What's the girl look like?"

"Sixteen, maybe seventeen. She was wearing jeans and a T-shirt. Black hair."

"Do you think the killer had her in the boat?"

Kyra shook her head. "Not from what I saw. Is the guy in the bedroom still alive?"

"No, he didn't have a chance."

"I didn't think he would even with immediate medical help. I've seen nasty gunshot wounds like he had, and they usually don't end well." Remembering the young man on the tile floor by the sliding glass door only reinforced why she left the police force. Six years ago she'd seen too much death and had needed to do something different. She'd still wanted to help make this world a safer place, but she couldn't continue investigating one murder after another. The Lord had something else in mind for her. Guardians, Inc. gave her the sense she was helping others without being personally involved in so much death.

Gabe began walking back toward the crime scene. "That's what I thought, but we called the local doctor who lives down the street to help. The victim died before Dr. Hunt could do anything."

"Michael Hunt, Ginny's little brother?"

"Yep, he's all grown up and has returned to Flamingo Cay to run the medical clinic. We've needed another doctor in town for quite some time."

The Michael Hunt she remembered used to follow her and Ginny, her best friend in high school, around generally making life difficult for them. She'd known from Ginny her little brother had gone on to be a doctor, but she hadn't seen him in years. The last time she'd heard about him, he'd been practicing in Chicago, so she hadn't thought she would see him in Flamingo Cay.

"Michael came back about four months ago."

As they neared the edge of the swamp, Kyra's tension returned, gripping her neck and fanning out along her shoulders. "I thought you were retiring."

"This is my last year."

She tilted her head. "Promise? When I was home for Dad's funeral, didn't you say that to me? I thought you meant it that time."

"Two years ago there wasn't anyone I felt could take over for me, but Wilson is a good man. He should do fine when I retire."

Kyra emerged from the heavy foliage that marked the beginning of the swamp that made up the Everglades. Flamingo Cay, not too far from Naples, was between the Glades and the Gulf of Mexico with its many islands off Florida's western coast.

She caught sight of a large man over six feet tall carrying a black bag, standing on the side deck off the bedroom talking to an officer. At that moment Michael glanced over his shoulder at her. For a few seconds their gazes linked across the yard. Then recognition dawned on his face, and he smiled at her, two dimples appearing and bringing back more memories of her childhood. Even as a kid he'd had a great smile—one that drew people to him.

"Tell me what happened here." Gabe paused in the side yard, returning her attention to the problem at hand.

Kyra reluctantly wrenched her look from Michael Hunt. "I was out on the beach after my aunt left to go walk with a friend at the track. I'd taken my towel and beach bag out there to just enjoy the sunrise and read and relax. Before I had a chance, I heard muffled gunshots. A young man stumbled out onto the beach from the Pattersons' backyard, collapsed and mumbled something about helping them, then died. I knew someone else was in trouble. I had my gun, so I called 911 and went to see if I could help."

"You might not be a detective anymore, but it's hard to get it out of your system."

"Instinct. I was a cop for a lot of years."

"Can you tell me anything else about the girl besides age and hair color?"

"She's pale, not much of a tan, with heavily made-up eyes in black. The color of them, though, was blue. When she glanced up at me, she looked so scared. But she kept going, which saved her life. The killer got off a shot, but she disappeared down the deck steps. I didn't see which way she went because I was focused on the assailant in the hallway. He never came into the room. He might have sensed me there. Maybe he saw a reflection in the sliding glass door. I don't know. I checked the rooms down the hallway, and that's when I found the other victim. Then I saw the killer running toward the swamp. I felt I had to go after him in case he was pursuing the girl."

Gabe rubbed his chin. "Hmm. The teenage girl could be Amy, Michael's younger sister."

"The one Ginny was raising until she went to the Philippines as a missionary?" Her childhood friend's little sister? If anything had happened to the girl, she would have been at a loss how to tell Ginny.

"Yup. Amy said she would run away before she'd go to the Philippines. She wanted to finish high school this coming year in Flamingo Cay. Michael agreed to come home and take care of her."

Kyra slanted her glance toward Michael striding toward them. His medium-length black hair lay at odd angles as though he'd run his hand through it multiple times. Even from a distance his blue eyes, so much like the teenage girl's when Kyra thought about it, lured her in. Compelling. Captivating. Even better than his smile. She dragged her attention away from his gaze, fastening it onto the cleft in his chin, then his full lips, which were tugged in a look of concern.

Gabe greeted Michael with a handshake. "Thanks for coming."

"I was too late. I don't think there was anything I could have done, though." Michael's look shifted to her. "Kyra Morgan?"

She nodded. "It's been a long time."

"Sixteen years. I think the last time I saw you was the summer right before I went to college. It's good to see you." He held out his hand to her.

She fit hers in his clasp, and his large fingers surrounded hers. The connection, warm, full of strength, further surprised her. "How's Ginny doing? I haven't heard from her since she went to the Philippines."

"Getting settled in." A smile leaked through the tired lines about his eyes and mouth, and he wiped moisture off his brow. "I forgot how bad the humidity could get here, especially in the summer. It takes some getting used to."

"I know. I had planned on spending a lot of time in the water to counter that."

Gabe cleared his throat. "I hate to break up this little reunion, but Michael, where is Amy?"

"At home. Why?"

Gabe fully faced Michael. "She may have been involved with what went down here."

Michael's tanned features paled. "No, that's not possible. Amy wouldn't hurt anyone. She won't even eat meat because animals are being killed to provide it."

"I saw a teenage girl fleeing from the house. She had blood on her hands and shirt."

Michael shook his head. "Not Amy."

Gabe pointed toward the house. "The person dead on the beach is Preston Stevens. Hasn't Amy been seeing him?"

"Not lately. She promised me." Panic seized Michael's cobalt-blue eyes.

"I want Kyra to meet her. If it's not the same girl she saw in the bedroom, then that's the end of it. If Amy was there, I need to talk to her. She's the only one left to tell us what happened before Kyra came on the scene," Gabe said using his usual laid-back approach, all the while assessing his surroundings and the situation.

She wanted to reassure Michael about his sister, to wipe that apprehensive expression from his face. "I don't think she had anything to do with either killing. The girl I saw was scared. The assailant I chased into the swamp shot at her but didn't hit her."

Michael gritted his jaws together so tightly a nerve jerked in his cheek. "Fine. I'm sure this is all a mistake." A vulnerability beneath his words infused his voice with doubt.

"You said she's at home. There's no time like the present to get this straightened out." Gabe started around to the back of the house and the beach, skirting Connors, who was with Preston's body, putting up crime-scene tape while another officer was talking to some of the neighbors outside.

Michael hung back, opening and closing his hands at his sides. He peered at Preston lying faceup on the beach, then back at Kyra.

She approached him. "You're not so sure, are you?"

He shook his head, bleakness in his eyes. "Not the way Amy has been acting lately. The first month I was back here everything was all right. Then at the start of the summer, she began to change into the little sister that Ginny warned me about."

"What?"

"Wild, rebellious, stubborn."

"Some of that describes a typical teenager. I can remember some of the things I pulled with Ginny." She grinned. "And you took pleasure in letting your mom know all about it."

For a fleeting second humor flashed into his eyes until his gaze fixed upon a point down the beach. Kyra turned and saw Gabe waiting for them four houses down.

"When we get this all straightened out, I hope we can talk." Michael began walking. "The one thing I know about Amy is she wouldn't hurt anyone. Just last week a bird flew into the glass window. She had me out there trying to revive it. I kept telling her I was a doctor for humans, not birds."

Kyra fell into step next to him as he passed near the crime-scene tape. "Did the bird make it?"

For a long moment Michael didn't say anything, only stared at Preston, a dark shadow in his eyes. Finally he blinked, shook his head slightly and focused on Kyra. "Yes, Twitter flew off an hour later as if nothing had happened."

"Twitter?"

"Amy named the bird that. Now do you see why I don't think she could have been involved? It had to be someone else."

"Sometimes people get caught up in something they never intended." Kyra touched his arm and stopped on the beach, compelling him to do likewise. "I used to investigate homicides for a living."

"Yeah, Ginny told me."

"You talked to Ginny about me?"

"You were Ginny's best friend, even if you two didn't get to see each other much in the past few years."

"I don't know about y'all, but I have a lot to do," Gabe shouted, his fists on his hips, his glare directed at them.

"I forgot how impatient he can be," Kyra said with a laugh and continued her trek toward the police chief. "My point in telling you that is if Amy is involved I might be able to help you." The second the words were out of her mouth, Kyra wanted to snatch them back. Help Michael? How?

She was only going to be here a week. Besides, what business was it of hers? She had so needed a break finally. Gabe was quite capable of finding the killer without her help.

"This little reunion will have to wait, y'all. Where's Amy?" Gabe charged up the back steps to the deck and waited at the door while his foot tapped against the wooden planks. "We haven't had a murder in Flamingo Cay in four years, and now I've got two in one day."

Michael reached around Gabe and opened one of the double glass doors. "She went to her bedroom. I'll go get her. Have a seat." He waved toward the den, then headed down the hall.

Before going into Michael's place, Kyra slipped off her swamp-soaked tennis shoes and strode to the outside water faucet and rinsed the mud off her legs and sneakers. After setting them out to dry, she entered the house.

Gabe removed his ball cap and scratched his thinning hair. "I've got a bad feeling about this." Then he plopped the hat—a sore subject with the town council, which thought he should wear his complete uniform—back on his head.

"Why do you say that?" Kyra asked as the sound of rushed footsteps resonated down the corridor.

A second later Michael appeared, his eyes huge, fear carving deep lines into his face. "She's not in there." He brought forward a bloody T-shirt. "But this was on the floor." His hand quavered as he thrust it toward Gabe.

"This is Amy's?" Gabe asked, making no move to take the article of clothing.

"Yes. She was wearing it yesterday."

Kyra headed toward the kitchen but paused in the entrance. "And this morning when you saw her?"

"I don't know. I didn't see what she had on. All I saw was a glimpse of her before Wilson called me."

"Where's a paper sack?" Kyra had known the Hunt family for years, and although she and Ginny didn't see each other in person much anymore, they did keep in touch by phone and email occasionally. Now she knew why she'd told Michael she would help—because of the years of friendship.

"In the top of the pantry. Why?" Michael clamped the edge of the T-shirt between his thumb and forefinger.

While she rummaged around in the pantry, Kyra heard Gabe explain about putting the shirt in the sack as evidence. When she found what she was looking for behind some pans, she returned to the living room. His forehead furrowed, Michael dropped the piece of clothing into the evidence bag.

"I need to take a look at the house. Is that okay?" Gabe asked, taking the sack.

Confusion clouding his eyes, Michael glanced from Gabe to Kyra. She gave him a nod, and he said, "Yes."

"Kyra, do you want to help?" Gabe crossed toward the hallway. "I could always use an extra pair of eyes. In fact, I could hire you as a consultant so you could work this case. I could use your expertise as a homicide detective. Besides, you've seen more murders than me, and one of my officers is on vacation."

"How about the sheriff and his deputies or the state police?"

"I'll put a call in for some help, but I don't know how much I'll get until next week. They're gonna be busy on St. Cloud Island. A big symposium on terrorism is being held there soon with some world leaders attending. I think something else is happening on Marco Island. Some big conference with the governor."

She couldn't turn down Gabe's request when he was the reason she'd become a police officer in the first place. "Sure, if you need me, I'll help but you don't have to hire me as a consultant. I'll poke around and see what I can come up with." She twisted toward Michael, wanting to erase the worry from his face. "I didn't see a gun on the floor by the body, and I didn't see Amy with one. I think the only one who had a gun was the assailant."

He peered at her as though she were speaking a foreign language.

"Preston and the other guy were shot. So where's her gun if she shot them?" Kyra asked.

Michael's eyes brightened. "Yeah. But why did she run away?"

"She was scared. People often react without thinking. Do you know any reason why she would go to the Pattersons' house?"

He shook his head, the light dimming again in his eyes.

She closed the space between them. "I told Gabe I would help, and I will."

"My most immediate concern is finding Amy. If the man shot at her, then he may be after her."

She couldn't dispute that—it was a very real possibility. "He fled into the swamp."

"She loves the swamp. What if he was going after her?"

His every word held such alarm that Kyra was drawn again to comfort Michael. She touched his arm, his bicep bunching beneath her fingertips. "The sequence of events doesn't support that. You were seeing her in this house while I was going after the killer."

"Then where did she go?"

"Good question. We need to find her." As Gabe disappeared down the hallway, Kyra inhaled deeply, smelling Michael's scent—musk and antiseptic. "While we're looking around, try calling her first then start calling her friends, if she doesn't answer her cell. See if she's with one of them or they know where she would go."

"I can do that." He dug into his pocket and withdrew his cell. "I also need to call my partner to tell him to cover for me for the next few days."

Kyra left him making the first call. She seriously doubted Amy was over at a friend's, but it gave Michael something to do while they searched the house. The person she'd seen running from the murder scene was frightened. What had Amy witnessed? What did Michael's sister know that caused the assailant to shoot at her? Could Amy ID the killer?

When she entered the teen's bedroom, Gabe closed a drawer. "I'm worried about Amy. If she witnessed a double homicide, the killer might not rest until he finds her."

"I agree." Kyra strolled toward a pegboard with photos pinned on it. She surveyed the array. "I haven't seen pictures of Amy since she was much younger. But this is definitely the girl I saw at the house." She tapped her finger at a girl in a photo in the center of the board—two girls, arms slung over each other's shoulders, huge smiles on their faces.

"That's Amy. I know that she has been in more trouble this past year than before, but I would never figure she would be involved in a murder even as a witness."

"Can you tell me anything about Preston? Why would someone want to kill him? Who is the other victim?" Kyra used the eraser end of a pencil to wake up Amy's computer. Amy's screen saver came blazing to life. A scene of a swamp—dark, eerie, with deep shadows except where a sunray burst through the thick foliage to light the murky water.

"Preston is—was a bit on the wild side. I've seen Amy and him together around town. I'm not sure who the other guy is. He must be passing through. Wilson is working on that."

"Could he have been involved in drugs?"

"Possibly. You think this is drug-related?"

"You know that drug dealers have used the Glades to smuggle in their poison so it's a very real possibility."

"Yeah, that's what I'm afraid of. A few years back I would have said Amy would never have been caught up in something like that. Now I can't."

"Which means she could be in deeper trouble than just the police looking for her to question her."

"Yup. The killer could be after her as a witness or a drug deal gone bad."

"It won't be the first time a murderer wants to silence a witness or a dealer wants to send a message about double-crossing him." Noticing Amy's internet server was still open, Kyra sat at the desk and punched some keys to bring up the girl's email account. She clicked on the last message Amy sent. "Gabe, come look at this." She peered over her shoulder at her mentor and glimpsed Michael standing in the doorway.

Both men approached the desk.

Michael hovered over Kyra to read, "I lost my cell at the cabin. He's got it. Gotta get out of here. Hide. Meet me at our place."

THREE

"He's got her cell? Who? How?" Michael's gut constricted. The throbbing in his head increased its tapping against his skull.

"Don't know." Kyra's gaze connected with Michael's. "Who's this person she's emailing called skullandcrossbones?"

"I would have said Preston, but he's dead. I don't know." Why didn't he? He'd tried to forge a bond with Amy, but— He couldn't think straight with Kyra's vanilla scent teasing his nostrils. When he'd been growing up, he'd fancied himself in love with Kyra, who thought of him only as Ginny's kid brother. But what did a boy of fifteen or sixteen really know about love? He didn't even think he had a good grasp on it now. Not after Sarah. He'd failed her when she'd needed him the most.

Gabe frowned. "Maybe that's something I could ask her friends."

"Let me do that. They might talk to me but not the police." Michael remembered the short list of

Amy's girlfriends he'd called and the fact he'd gotten nowhere with them. They knew something and weren't talking. But he had to do something to help Amy, and maybe after he pressed upon them the danger his sister was in, they would open up to him.

Indecision shadowed the police chief's eyes.

"He might have a point. I could go with Michael. See if I can figure out who's lying or telling the truth. I got pretty good at reading people while working as a detective in Dallas."

"Great, I'm glad you're gonna help me. Our resources are stretched at best on a good day. This isn't a good day. The officer who has some knowledge about computers is the one on vacation this week. He's not even in town. That leaves me with only Wilson, Connors and Nichols."

"That's also something I can help you with, Gabe. It's a necessity in my job. If it's okay with you and Michael, I can dig around and see what I can come up with on Amy's computer." Kyra peered from the police chief to him.

Her professional facade had descended, but this side of Kyra was just as appealing as the one who had declared she would help him. For months Michael had figured he was in over his head with Amy, but it was official now. Although he was only thirty-three, he felt decades older than his seventeen-year-old kid sister. "I don't have any problem with that. Chief?"

"Nope. Then that's settled. I'll leave it here for you to do whatever you do." Gabe headed for the door. "I don't see anything else in here that could help us find Amy." He paused at the door. "Michael, show me which way she would have come into the house the last time."

He panned the room, then joined Gabe in the hallway. "It had to be the back door through the kitchen."

"What's Amy's cell-phone number?" The police chief trailed behind Michael toward the kitchen.

Michael gave it to him and added, "Remember she doesn't have it with her." He surveyed the floor for any red spots on the tile, then when he didn't see any, he lifted his gaze to take in the rest of the room.

"Or so she wants us to think. We only have her word that 'he' has it."

"You think she wrote that in the email because she knew she could be tracked by the cell's GPS?"

"It's possible, but not probable," Gabe said, followed by a humorless chuckle. "We might be able to track the person who took Amy's cell if he has it as she said. I'll get Connors on it."

"Turn the tables on the guy Amy is running from?"

"Ain't technology great." Gabe winked and sauntered toward the back door.

Michael certainly hadn't had time to keep up with all the technology being developed—except in his field of medicine—with his work schedule. He was one of two doctors in a community with a large ratio of elderly people who needed a great deal of medical attention. And before he came back to Flamingo Cay, his life had been a living nightmare for the last year in Chicago. Still was. The image of Sarah at the accident that had taken her life continued to haunt him even after over a year. He hadn't been able to save her.

He wasn't going to lose his sister, too. "How are we going to find Amy? She's in trouble."

"Well, I guess we'll have to locate Amy the old-fashioned way."

"How?"

"We talk to her friends, check places that she goes to, and I know someone who has a bloodhound that's a pretty good tracker. I'll give Harvey a call and have him bring Boomer to track Amy's movements when she left here. Maybe we can locate her that way."

Hunt his sister down like a fugitive? The thought knotted his gut into a tight, hard ball. "Whatever you think is best. I just know we need to get to her before the killer does."

"Can you get me something that she's worn lately?"

"Sure." Michael made his way back to Amy's

bedroom. When he entered, Kyra peered up at him and smiled. "Find anything?" he asked.

"A few things. She's gotten a couple of emails from this skullandcrossbones person during the past few weeks, mostly chatter about Preston. Before that nothing. Maybe the person is a new friend. Do you remember her talking about someone she'd befriended recently?"

"No. But then she and I didn't talk all that much, especially lately. She sulked a lot. When I asked her what was wrong, she denied anything was." He waved his hand toward the Patterson house. "Obviously that wasn't true." He strode to a pile of shirts and shorts lying next to Amy's empty dirty-clothes hamper. "Gabe is going to try and track her with a dog."

"That's good. She's in danger. She may not think coming in to the police is the best solution to her problem, but it is."

"Why wouldn't she turn herself in to the police?"

"I don't know. Maybe she will when she has time to stop and think clearly. Right now she is in flight mode."

He grabbed a shirt Amy had worn recently. "If we find her, would you be willing to be her bodyguard? Ginny told me about your company, and if a killer is after Amy, we'll need the services of a good bodyguard. As Gabe said, he's understaffed.

I know you agreed to help the chief, but Amy's safety is the most important thing right now."

She opened her mouth to say something but snapped it closed. Pressing her lips together, she glanced away for a moment then reestablished eye contact. "I don't normally act as a bodyguard myself, but yes, I'll help. I'll protect her if it comes to that."

For the first time in a while he didn't feel so alone dealing with his problems. "Thanks. This is so out of my league. I'm glad you decided to come home this week." He held up the article of clothing. "I'd better get this to Gabe. Maybe we'll have Amy home by the end of the day."

Kyra watched him leave. The expression of hope on his face tore at her composure. She'd been involved with disappearances of teenagers before and so many of them didn't turn out well. She owed it to Ginny and even Michael to find their sister and then protect her. She couldn't leave at the end of the week, go back to Dallas and forget what was happening unless there was a resolution to Amy's troubles.

Mentally she began making plans to call her secretary, then see if Elizabeth Caulder could cover for her if she was in Flamingo Cay longer than a week. What else did she need to do? A lot of that would depend on what happened with Amy. The thought she wouldn't be found left Kyra cold in the midst of the summer heat. She would do what she could to make the outcome different.

She clicked on Amy's icon for trash to see what she'd deleted lately. A blank screen greeted Kyra's perusal. Amy had emptied her trash. It would take her a little longer, but files weren't completely deleted off the computer until there was no more space and a file was written over a trashed one.

Later that morning, Kyra found Michael on the deck facing the Gulf. The blue water glittered as though thousands of shards of crystal had been strewn over its surface. "I didn't know how much I misssed this until I came home."

Gripping the railing, Michael hunched his shoulders and leaned farther into it. "I know that's the way I felt when I came back here." His look didn't stray from the stretch of sea no more than a hundred yards away. "I remember once when I was twelve and found an old dinghy. I worked all summer to get it in shape. I had planned to go all the way to Key West in it." He slid her a smile that vanished in a second. "I didn't make it more than twenty or so feet offshore before I began to sink. I hadn't repaired all the holes in the bottom, at least not well enough that they didn't leak. That boat might still be out there somewhere." He pointed in the direction of where it had gone down.

She came up next to him, fighting the urge to

cover his hand on the railing with hers. The wistful tone in his voice made her ache for a time when they hadn't had any real worries. "You haven't swum out there to see it?"

"No. When I got here, I hit the ground running and haven't stopped since. My partner and I are very busy." A deep sigh escaped his lips. "I should know what was going on with Amy, too. I feel like I've let her down, and now she's in trouble."

This time she did touch his upper arm, drawing his full attention. Although her gesture was an act of comfort, she felt strange because she found herself attracted to a man who was a good friend's kid brother—one she had dealt with as a young teenage boy with a crush on her. "Ginny was having problems with Amy. She hit sixteen, and according to your sister, Amy changed overnight."

He shifted toward her, her hand dropping to her side. "Did you find anything on her computer to help find her?"

"The name on the email account of skullandcrossbones is a Kip Thomas. Do you know someone by that name?"

"No."

"I've asked Gabe to see what he can find out about this person who supposedly lives in Naples. It could be a fake name and address. That's not hard to do when setting up an email account."

"Good. Anything else?"

"A journal she kept up until ten days ago. She deleted it, but I was able to recover it. Did something happen at that time?"

A faraway look darkened his blue eyes to a storm. "That's when I grounded her for coming in two hours late from a date. She'd just gotten off from being grounded a few days ago."

"Who did she go out with?"

"She told me Brady Lawson, a guy she used to date during the school year, but I'm pretty sure it was Preston. I didn't see the car she came home in, but I heard it. It sounded like Preston's GTO. Lately she has been going out with Preston, and she knew I didn't think he was the right kind of guy for her." He rotated around and sat back on the railing, folding his arms over his chest. "Did you read the journal?"

"Yes, a lot of angst. Brady and she broke up two months ago, then she met another guy she thought was hot."

"Did she say who?"

"No. She called him Hottie. Apparently they spent time in the swamp, partying."

"That Preston." His features strengthened into a scowl. "But I don't know for sure and that's the problem." A nerve twitched in his cheek.

"She talked a lot about a girl named Laurie. Do you know her?"

"Yes, Laurie and Amy were BFFs, or so she told me on a number of occasions."

"Then I suggest we go talk to her best friend first."

"Right now?"

"No, after Gabe searches the area with the bloodhound. I figure you'll want to be here in case he turns up anything useful."

"Yes. Maybe the dog will find Amy's trail and lead us right to her." Hope flared in his expression for a few seconds.

"If nothing is found to help us, we can go talk to Laurie. She might know something about where Amy would go if she was afraid."

"Frankly the place I would say she would go was Laurie's, but when I called earlier no one answered the phone." Michael shuddered, his shoulders drooping. "This is a peaceful little town. A kid shouldn't have to be afraid for her life."

"No, but sadly that's not the way it is in this world."

"Yeah, there are two dead young men to prove that. I saw my fair share of gunshot victims in the emergency room in Chicago. Some were caught up in gang wars. Others in drug deals gone bad. I thought I had left that behind."

"As a police officer, I discovered evil can exist anywhere."

"Wilson told me he didn't know who the other

victim at the Pattersons' house was. He appeared older than Preston. Do you think this has anything to do with drugs or something like that?"

"Maybe. When I talked to Gabe a few minutes ago, he told me the other person who died at the scene was Preston's cousin from Miami, Tyler Stevens. His cousin had been visiting and hadn't been here long. He had the same black dagger tattooed on his neck as Preston did."

"A gang?"

"Gabe is checking with the Miami police."

He pushed away from the railing. "I never thought of Flamingo Cay and gangs in the same context."

"He said they checked where the man I chased ran into the undergrowth and saw another set of prints near his and mine. Looked to be about a size-thirteen shoe, Gabe said. Since it rained last night, he thinks either someone was standing there watching the house or waiting for Amy or someone else."

A gray tinge to his face, Michael sucked in a shaky breath then slowly released it. "Let's see what progress Harvey and his bloodhound, Boomer, have made. Maybe they've already found a trail that will lead us right to Amy."

Kyra hoped so, too, but what she wouldn't voice to Michael was her concern over how they would find Amy. When his gaze snagged hers as he moved toward his back door, though, she glimpsed the same fear in his expression as she had. Amy could be dead somewhere nearby. Like the two young men at the Pattersons'.

She halted Michael's progress into his house with, "Amy came back and changed. She was alive a while ago and got away from whoever killed those boys because I chased him to the canal in the opposite direction from here. I don't think she had time to come home, change and somehow end up in the swamp being chased by the assailant."

Pain glazed his eyes. "Yeah, but what if the second person Gabe found the prints of followed her here and waited until she left again?"

"With all the police around here? Probably not." At least she prayed he hadn't. Kyra grabbed her damp tennis shoes and put them on.

Frowning, Michael yanked open the back door and strode through the entrance and continued toward the foyer. When he stepped outside onto the porch, he peered toward the Pattersons' house. A red, beat-up truck was parked behind a police cruiser in the driveway. "Where's Gabe? Harvey?"

The need to let him know he wasn't alone inundated her. This was someone she'd grown up with, and she'd been at his house playing with his older sister. "It looks like Gabe has already started tracking Amy's movements."

Michael turned to the left in the direction Kyra

indicated. Gabe ambled across the next-door neighbor's yard, slightly behind a large man with a barrel chest and a bloodhound in the lead. "I'm not ready for this." His voice caught on the last word as his fingers grasped the railing.

Kyra clasped his arm, wishing she'd been able to prevent Amy from running away this morning at the Pattersons'. But if Amy had stopped, the killer would have shot her in the back. "Remember I'm here for you. We'll find her, and I'll make sure she's safe."

He pried loose his grip from the railing and peered toward her. "I appreciate your help. I've never had something like this happen to me."

She was all too familiar with a person agonizing over the disappearance of a loved one. "Most people thankfully don't."

"Flamingo Cay is a small town. Things like this don't happen here. I know that Gabe has been the police chief for twenty-three years, but is he capable of handling these multiple murders?"

"I know for a fact he can. When I was thirteen, there had been a family murdered here not far outside of town. He wasn't the police chief yet, but he's the one who solved the case and brought the man in. A fine piece of detective work. He and Dad were friends. He used to come over, and I would overhear the details about the case. Of course, they didn't know I was listening. But that's when I started wanting to be a police officer."

"That must have been right before we moved to Flamingo Cay."

"Yeah, if I remember correctly you all moved in a couple of months after that case was solved."

"Still, I'm glad you're helping him with the case. Ginny told me about some of the murders you worked on in Dallas."

The idea he and Ginny had talked about her warmed her face. Yes, she'd talked about Michael with Ginny, but she had also discussed Amy. A friend curious about a friend's family.

He shoved away from the railing and descended the steps. "I wonder if he's checked the swamp area behind the Pattersons' place."

"He probably will after he finds Amy's trail. I didn't see anything while I was in the swamp that would point to who the killer is, but then I was ducking bullets."

Michael clamped his jaw tightly, his neck stiff. "You make it sound like it was no big deal."

"It is a big deal, but I refuse to let it get to me or I'll hesitate when I shouldn't." She descended the front steps. "You said Amy loves the swamp. Any particular place she liked to go?"

"She had a kayak she kept sometimes at the old pier at the end of the trail, but usually at the public dock off Main. She asked me about a few places, but I never heard about one area she spent all her time. She gave me some story that she needed to help preserve places like the Everglades and that she liked moving around."

"Why don't you think she meant it?"

"There was something in her tone. A certain look on her face. She kept her gaze averted. Just a feeling." He headed across the yard toward Gabe and Harvey.

The police chief came to a halt at the curb in front of Michael's house and removed a toothpick from his mouth. "We followed a trail across several neighbors' yards until it reached the middle of Bay Shore Drive and suddenly ended like someone had picked her up in a car. I've called Nichols and Connors to check with friends and to begin a search of the town. What was she doing yesterday? Who was she with?"

"Amy loves spending time in the marshes."

"So she spent most of yesterday in the swamp?" Gabe rolled the toothpick between his thumb and forefinger as he started toward the Pattersons' house. "Alone?"

"She never mentioned anyone, but I think Laurie sometimes went with her." Michael pointed toward the thick cluster of trees edging the undergrowth.

As they came closer to the border of the swamp, Harvey quickened his pace, following behind his bloodhound. They entered where the killer had when Kyra went after him, not on the well-worn path ten yards away.

"Let's see where Boomer takes us. Since it's summer there's a lot of water." Gabe peered at Kyra's tennis shoes. "You might want to wear something else."

"I don't have anything else. And as you can see, I've been in mud up to my ankles. Don't worry about me."

Harvey directed Boomer into the underbrush with Gabe trailing next, then Kyra and Michael. With nose to the ground, the bloodhound took off, charging through the vegetation in the same direction Kyra had gone only hours ago after the assailant.

They emerged from the undergrowth onto the path, and Michael fell in right behind her. "When I was a child, I use to come here like Amy. Loved the adventure. That's why I really couldn't say much to Amy about coming here alone. But I've been back for four months and have only gone into the swamp a few times."

"Things change when we grow up. I can't say I liked exploring the swamp when I was a child."

One corner of his mouth tilted up. "And now all of a sudden you do?"

The rotting smell of vegetation coupled with the incessant noise of insects brought back childhood memories. "Maybe I should amend my earlier statement. Some things change. That isn't one of them. I prefer pursuing an adventure somewhere else. At the moment somewhere air-conditioned." Beads of perspiration rolled down Kyra's face, blurring her vision for a second until she blinked to clear it.

Michael swiped a hand across his damp forehead. "I haven't gotten used to the humidity yet either, and it's been four months."

When Boomer approached the short pier, the dog lumbered over the wooden planks, some broken and missing, going back and forth from one side to the other until he reached the end. The bloodhound stopped and sat, looking up at Harvey as if to say this was as far as he would go.

"Good boy." Harvey scratched behind Boomer's ears.

Michael went to the edge and leaned over. "Amy's kayak isn't here so she must have it at the town dock."

"One- or two-man?" With her hand shielding her eyes, Kyra scanned the open waterway that stretched across a few hundred yards to more tangled vegetation, one mangrove island after another. Where did the killer go? Who was the second man? Why had the man killed Preston and Tyler?

"Two, like my kayak I keep there."

"I'll have Wilson check to see if her kayak is at the dock. Someone could have given her a ride there. If it's gone, then we'll need to search the swamp for Amy." Gabe dropped the chewed-up toothpick into the top pocket of his shirt.

Harvey took off his beat-up straw hat and mopped his face with a handkerchief, then stuffed it back into his jeans. "I'll have Boomer check around the pier and see if he can come up with anything else." Harvey plopped his hat back on his head and indicated to Boomer to get up. "Then we'll head back along the path."

"So this was a waste of time." What had Amy gotten caught up in? Michael went back over the past few days in his head, trying to remember anything she might have said to him to help them find her. He'd been gone a lot because his partner had been on vacation. Thankfully his partner had got back yesterday evening and could fill in for Michael this morning at the clinic. But that consolation didn't give him the answers he needed.

"No, not totally. We know wherever Amy went she used a car most likely. Yeah, it would have been nice to have Boomer lead us to her." Gabe waved his hand toward Harvey and his dog beginning their trip back to Pelican Lane. "I'm heading to the station. We need to expand our search of the town and see if Amy's kayak is at the public pier."

Michael stared at the canal gently flowing past the old pier. The water's smooth surface—like a mirror—reflected the nearby trees in it. A breeze blew the scent of overripe, damp vegetation to his nostrils. Every shade of green from a light yellow-ish tint to a dark vibrant one met his inspection of the terrain.

Amy, where are you? Are you safe? In the past he would have prayed to the Lord, but for months he'd been silent. He pivoted to go back and nearly collided with Kyra behind him.

His hand shot out to steady her. Automatically he brought her closer, her feminine scent driving the aromas of the swamp into the background and totally centering his focus on the beautiful woman with her auburn hair pulled back from her face. That only emphasized her large eyes, a golden-brown like dark honey. "I'm sorry."

She chuckled. "The last place I'd want to end up is in that water." Her gaze shifted to a hole in the plank at the canal below. "I wasn't like you and Amy. I didn't go exploring much. Put me in the rough section of a town at night, and I'd feel more comfortable."

A shiver flowed from her, through his hands and up his arms, making him acutely aware that his teenage fantasy girl was standing before him. His attention latched on to her mouth, so close that his long-ago dreams of kissing Kyra overwhelmed him. Throwing him completely off guard. He stepped back, the heel of one foot coming down a couple of inches over the end of the pier.

He teetered a few seconds. She reached out to catch him before he went into the water. He managed to regain his balance and sidled away before he made a total fool of himself. He'd been serious about Sarah in Chicago. They had planned to marry until a man fell asleep at the wheel of his car and had hit them. Despite his injuries, Michael had tried to save Sarah, but all his medical knowledge hadn't kept her from slipping away from him only minutes after he'd manage to get to her in the wrecked car. The pain in her eyes, the last shuddering breath she'd taken still tormented him.

"Good recovery." Her beautiful mouth formed a heart-melting smile that touched a coldness he'd been encased in for over a year.

"Let's leave before we both end up in the water." He allowed her to go first toward the path that led through the grove of trees. "I remember when this pier was in good shape and used by a lot of the neighbors on Pelican Lane. But a couple of hurricanes have taken their toll on it. I think Amy is one of the few who still use it from time to time."

"Has much else changed about the town?"

"Its population has grown to three thousand. Other than that, no." But then he hadn't really paid a lot of attention. He'd thrown himself into his new job, relieved that the pace was a bit slower than a Chicago hospital but enough that he didn't dwell on his past. He'd needed that. Or so he thought.

Maybe his emotional distancing had brought all this on. The pace might have been slower, but it hadn't stopped him from working long hours rather than face his feelings head-on.

Harvey, Gabe and Boomer stood off the trail near the edge of it.

Kyra approached them. "What did the dog find?"

"Several cigarette butts." Gabe took out an evidence bag, stooped and eased the filter ends into the small manila envelope. "May be nothing. May be important."

Standing, he studied the ground around him a long moment, then ambled behind Boomer and Harvey. The bloodhound went to the side deck.

"That's probably the way the assailant went into the house," Kyra said while the trio made their way to Gabe's patrol car.

"By the time DNA testing comes back on the cigarette butts, Amy could be dead."

"It can take a while even with a rush on it, but it could help make a case against the guy when he is found."

"That might be too late for my sister." When Michael emerged from the undergrowth onto the road near the Pattersons' house, he saw Gabe on his cell. Harvey was pulling away in his old pickup truck with Boomer in the back, looking at Michael.

"Officer Connors just called to tell me he's

checked all Amy's usual haunts and found nothing. No one has seen her."

"How about Laurie?" Kyra asked, looking down at her muddy tennis shoes for the second time that day.

"Connors said no one answered when he called her house about an hour ago. He even drove by and didn't see Mrs. Carson's white Chevy out front. Since she works evenings, he thought she might be there and was sleeping or something."

"If anyone knows where Amy is it would be Laurie. Where one goes the other usually isn't far behind." Michael stuffed his hands into his front jean pockets, his shoulders slumping forward. He needed to do something. He couldn't sit around and just wait. He'd never been good at doing that. He looked for solutions to problems and carried them out—or at least he had until he hit an emotional wall with Sarah's death. "What can I do to help?"

"Gabe, maybe Michael and I could go to Laurie's and see if she or her mother are home yet. That way you can use all your men for the search."

"Fine. As I told you before, I can use any help I can get. Call if you find out anything." Gabe opened his car door and climbed inside.

"I will." The sun's rays tinted Kyra's cheeks a rosy color.

"You said something about expanding the search.

Are you going to search the swamp?" Michael glimpsed a patrol car coming down the street.

"I haven't heard back from Wilson yet. If Amy's kayak is gone at the Main Street dock, yes. If not, we should concentrate on the town and the surrounding area. Since someone most likely picked her up in a car, that's probably how she's traveling."

"Laurie has a car. Amy's Camry is still in the garage." He prayed it was Laurie who had come and picked Amy up. The alternative could mean his sister was dead like the two young men.

"If Laurie isn't there, at least check with Mrs. Carson to see if her car is gone." Gabe kneaded the cords of his neck. "Or look into the garage. If I remember correctly, there's a window that allows you to see inside. But you didn't hear that from me."

Kyra chuckled. "I never heard a word."

Michael kept thinking about the swamp, the lure of the slow-moving water. "What if she didn't use her kayak but someone else's?"

"We'll explore the swamp even if her kayak is at the dock, but that kind of search requires a lot of manpower and coordination. I couldn't get it together before dark. If nothing turns up, we'll start tomorrow morning. I'll put the call in to the sheriff's department about the possibility. Maybe they can spare a few people to help."

"Fine," Michael said between gritted teeth.

Gabe ambled over to Nichols, who had parked

and was getting out of his car. The police chief spoke to his officer, then the young man got back in the cruiser and left. Gabe took his cell out and made a call.

Michael pulled out his car keys. "I'll drive."

"Maybe I should wash my shoes again or change."

"Don't worry. I'll clean the car after this is all over with." He pointed down at his boots. "I feel like the clock is ticking on this."

"Fine, I understand." Kyra slipped into his car as he did. "Is it just Laurie and her mother?"

"Yes, Laurie lives with only her mother. If Laurie is anything like Amy in the summer, she's sleeping in. Usually Amy isn't up until ten or eleven." He started the Saturn's engine. Before backing out, he twisted toward Kyra. "Should I call Laurie first? See if she's there. It could be a wasted trip, like Officer Connors's."

"No. If she's home, I'd like to see her reaction when she finds out about Amy going missing. I might be able to tell if she knows anything and isn't saying."

FOUR

"Let's just hope we find Laurie at home and she can lead us to Amy." Slowly over the course of the past few hours, the muscles in Kyra's shoulders and neck had knotted until now pain streaked down her back. She didn't have a good feeling about this but didn't want to worry Michael any more than he already was. "Tell me about Amy. The last time I saw her she was a little girl. When my dad died and I came home for the funeral, she'd been at church camp."

"I don't think she has stepped foot in a church in the past year, which distressed Ginny to no end."

"But not you?"

His hands about the steering wheel tightened, his knuckles white. "Let's just say I have my own issues with the Lord." He inhaled a deep breath and blew it out slowly. "In a few weeks she'll start her senior year at Flamingo High School."

"How are her grades this past year?"

"Good. Mostly Bs with a few As."

"So, no problems at school?"

"Ginny told me there were a couple of girls harassing her at the beginning of her junior year, but by the time I'd arrived here in April, everything seemed to be taken care of."

"How about her friends? Do you approve of them?"

"That's been the main problem. Preston's reputation isn't—wasn't good. He was wild, always partying. He graduated this year and has been picking up odds jobs this summer. He lived with his older brother—actually not far from where Laurie's house is."

"Has Preston lived here all his life?"

"No, he moved here from Miami at the beginning of the school year. I was trying to give Amy room to see what kind of person he was. I remember when Mom told Ginny she couldn't date that guy in high school."

So did Kyra. She'd helped Ginny sneak out of the house to go out with Danny. Ginny had been determined to date him in spite of what her mother had said. She was seventeen and should be able to pick her own boyfriends. "You knew about her seeing Danny?"

"Yeah. I saw her one night climbing back into the house."

"And you didn't say anything to your parents?"

"I'd grown out of my tattle-telling stage. I didn't

want Amy to sneak out against my wishes and look what has happened." He turned onto Sunshine Avenue. "Preston's is the third house on the left. Laurie lives several down from there."

As they passed Preston's home and the police cruiser parked out front, Kyra studied the plain, white place with a yard that was mostly dirt and dead plants. One eight-foot crepe myrtle with dark pink blooms draped all over it stood sentinel at the side by the driveway, the only color in an otherwise drab setting. A Harley Davidson motorcycle sat close to the sidewalk near the porch.

As Michael came to a stop at the end of the block, he closed his eyes for a few seconds, his hands opening and closing around the steering wheel. "The past few months haven't been easy for me or Amy. Getting to know each other. Learning to live together. She hasn't wanted to accept my authority as her guardian. I had no experience at parenting when I arrived. I feel I have even less now. Amy has blocked my attempts every step of the way."

"That can be typical. Challenging authority isn't uncommon. According to Ginny, you did your fair share as a teenager. I seem to remember you going with some friends to Tampa against your mother's wishes."

"Yeah, I was grounded for a month when she found out." Climbing from his car, he peered at her over the top of the gray Saturn. "It's disconcerting to have someone know all about my childhood pranks."

"Just wanting to get you to remember how it was." Although Michael had his share of childhood antics, he'd become a doctor who'd changed his plans to help Ginny when she was given an opportunity to fulfill a lifetime dream of serving as a missionary overseas for two years. So far she liked what she'd seen of Ginny's kid brother.

"So when I find Amy, I won't ground her for the rest of her life?"

Kyra laughed. "Something like that."

When Michael reached the porch, he rang the doorbell while Kyra assessed the surroundings. Laurie's house needed a coat of blue paint, but otherwise the place was kept up, the lawn mowed and the weeds pulled. Several minutes passed, and Michael pressed the bell again.

A white Chevy parked in the driveway made Kyra suspicious. The hairs on her nape prickled. She swiveled her attention toward the front picture window and glimpsed a curtain fall back into place.

"I guess no one's home." Michael swung around and frowned at the white car. "That's Cherie Carson's car," he said in a low voice. "So where is she? At a neighbor's?"

Kyra opened the screen and banged on the door. "Someone is home."

Thirty seconds later, a petite woman with medium-length brown hair peeked out from a crack of no more than a couple of inches and said, "Yes?"

"Mrs. Carson, we're here to talk to your daughter. Is she home?" The overpowering scent of roses assailed Kyra's nostrils.

The lady's mouth pinched together, her eyebrows slashing downward. "Who are you?"

Before Kyra could show the woman her identification, Michael stepped forward, his shoulder brushing up against Kyra's. "Hi, Cherie. It's important that we have a word with Laurie. Amy is missing."

Cherie Carson's eyes grew round. "Laurie isn't here."

"Where is she?" Kyra asked after a few seconds' silence.

The woman clutched the edge of the door, still only open a few inches. "She's at her aunt's in Tampa and won't be back until the weekend."

"We need to talk to her." Michael grasped Kyra's hand and held it. His tension conveyed his tone.

"I can call Laurie later and let her know. But I don't know when I'll be able to get hold of her. My sister and her were going to do some shopping today. I'll have her call you, Michael." Cherie started to close the door.

He reached out to stop her from doing it. "Please. This is important. I think Amy is in trouble, and if Laurie knows anything—"

"I'm so sorry to hear about Amy, but Laurie has been gone. Knowing your sister, she'll show up soon with some wild story. Goodness me, she certainly has dragged Laurie into enough escapades. Now if you'll excuse me, I've got a splitting headache and was lying down." The woman's grip on the door tightened so much her fingertips reddened.

Michael took a half step forward. "Laurie may know where she would have gone."

Pain blinked in and out of the woman's expression. "Check with her other friends. Laurie doesn't know." She moved back quickly and slammed the door shut, the lock clicking into place.

Michael squeezed Kyra's hand, transmitting his tension, before releasing his hold. "She's never been very friendly but this is…" His words grounded to a halt.

"It doesn't look like we'll get anywhere. Maybe Gabe can."

He let the screen bang closed. His glare drilled into the wire mesh.

Kyra descended the porch stairs. "Is she that way with everyone?"

Michael pivoted and accompanied her toward the car. "Amy assured me after my first run-in with the woman she was that way with all men and not to take it personally. It seems her husband left her a few years back. Didn't come home from work but called her the next day to tell her it was over."

What was it with married couples? First her mother walked out on her dad when she was ten. Her father had been devastated. She had been too, but she'd spent the next year consoling her dad. He was never the same after her mother left. "Something like that happened to my older sister who lives in Boston now. Except thankfully she didn't have any children to worry about." And that was why she wouldn't marry. She had seen too many broken marriages to want one for herself. Her job was her life and that was the way she wanted it.

After Michael settled in the front seat and started his car, he pulled away from the curb. "Why didn't you ever marry?"

"Who said I didn't?"

"I assumed since Ginny never said anything about it to me that you hadn't."

"Do you two make it a habit of talking about me a lot?" The fact Ginny and Michael might have made Kyra feel strange. When his attention zeroed in on her face, she grinned. "Don't you know it's not good to gossip?"

A smile touched his blue eyes, sparkling them. "We never *gossiped* about you. I inquired about how you were doing from time to time. That's all."

She wouldn't tell him that she'd asked about him once. After his older sister kidded her about robbing the cradle, she'd never asked again. Ginny was right. There was five years' difference between them. Kyra fastened her gaze on his strong jawline, wanting to know about this man. Did he feel like she did about marriage? Was his job his whole life? "I didn't want to marry. Being a cop would have been hard on a marriage. How about you? Did you ever marry?"

For a few seconds a shadow flittered in and out of his eyes. "You mean Ginny never told you about me? I'm crushed."

Didn't Ginny mention that Michael was getting serious with a woman in Chicago, even thinking about marriage? What had happened? Her curiosity spiked. Did he marry the lady? Were they divorced?

He turned onto Pelican Lane, and all evidence of a smile vanished as he stared at the house at the end of the road.

She noticed Gabe's police cruiser was still at the Pattersons'. She'd thought he would have left by now. "You okay?"

"What am I supposed to do? Go back to the house and twiddle my thumbs?"

"Do people do that anymore?"

"Okay. Wear a path in my floor pacing."

"What do you want to do?"

He parked in his driveway. "Go looking for Amy. If the police are covering the town, then I'd like to go into the swamp. I know a couple of places where Amy has mentioned she's gone. I'd like to check those out. I'll have enough time before dark."

"No, *we'll* have enough time. I'm coming with you."

"Are you sure? Aren't you the lady who doesn't like swamps?"

"Swamps are fine. It's the snakes that inhabit them that I don't like."

"Alligators are all right, then?"

"Sure. They're big, and I can see them coming."

"Not always. They can hide under the water and surprise their prey."

"Are you trying to scare me away?"

"No, but I don't want to be responsible for anything happening to you."

Weariness infused each of his words and something else that Kyra couldn't quite grasp. Possibly regret? Guilt? As a police officer she'd had to deal with both those emotions quite a bit. "Oh, nothing's going to. I'm very capable of taking care of myself. I'm taking my gun."

"You carry a gun all the time?"

"When I think it's necessary, and it might be necessary in this case." She began to stroll toward her house. "I'll just be a sec."

Kyra ran up the stairs to the front porch and let

herself into the house. Rock-and-roll music blasted from the speakers in the great room, pulsating the air. Kyra smelled the faint odor of something burning. Aunt Ellen was cooking again. She did that when she was upset. With all the patrol cars on the street today, she couldn't blame her aunt for being agitated.

She hurried and washed her feet then grabbed a clean pair of shoes and popped into the kitchen to tell her aunt where she was going.

"Oh, dear, I've burned the cookies again. I was so looking forward to them." Her aunt donned her hot-pink mittens to take the baking sheet out of the oven. When she opened the door on the stove, dark gray smoke poured into the room.

"Aunt Ellen," Kyra called out over the noise of the music. "I'm going with Michael Hunt into the swamp." Her gaze glued to the charred pieces of cookies, she added, "Don't wait dinner for me."

Aunt Ellen opened the window above the sink and turned on the vent over the stove. "He's such a nice young man. I just hate what he's going through right now. I was going to make a second batch for him."

"Don't worry about it. You don't have to go to the trouble."

"Oh, no. I am." Aunt Ellen pitched the burned cookies into the sink and ran water over them, then reached for the mixing bowl. "It's no trouble.

Keeps my mind off what's been happening on our street. In the very house next door to us."

She crossed the kitchen and hugged her aunt. "Are you worried something will happen to you?"

"No, dearie. At the last Founder's Day shooting contest, I bested Gabe, and everyone knows he's the best shot in the area." She grinned. "Well, until that day." She slipped her hand into the large pocket on her hot-pink-and-white apron and pulled out a pistol. "I'll be all right. You go help Michael." She patted Kyra on the arm, then twisted around and began measuring flour. "You know, Michael is single. It's about time you got married."

Not in this lifetime, Kyra thought and hurried from the house. Her partner in the Dallas Police Department had struggled with his marriage for years. When his wife had asked for a divorce, he'd nearly lost his job over it because he'd started drinking heavily. She never wanted to be that emotionally connected to another person that her happiness depended on him. Her father had taught her to stand on her own two feet and protect her heart at all costs.

As she hurried toward Michael's house, he emerged from the front entrance. Anger shot out of his eyes. His gaze zeroed in on her and beneath the fury lurked fear.

"What's wrong?"

"Someone has been in Amy's bedroom while we were gone."

"Amy?"

"I don't know." He reentered his house and strode down the hall toward his sister's bedroom. "The window wasn't open like that when we left." Michael gestured toward the one across the room. "She has a key. Why would she come through the window? It's not like I was here and she would have to sneak in." His eyes stinging from lack of sleep, he rubbed his hands down his face. Not knowing what to think was putting it mildly. His head pounded with each attempt to make sense out of what was happening.

"Other than the window being open, do you see anything else out of place? Something gone?"

He slowly made a tour of Amy's bedroom, noting the usual disarray. When he came to the desk, he stiffened. "The laptop is gone." Hidden behind a stack of books on wildlife, the space where her computer usually sat was empty. "You left it in here, didn't you?"

Kyra closed the distance between them, a frown lining her forehead. "Yes. I was going to work some more on it later, then see what Gabe wanted to do with it."

"Why would someone take it?"

"Maybe there's something on it the killer didn't want us to see. There was a folder of photos she deleted I wanted to go through as well as another one still on her hard drive."

"Or maybe it was Amy and she didn't want us to see something." He plowed both hands through his hair. "But that doesn't make sense. None of this does to me."

"As you said, she could have used her key. Why come through the window? I hadn't had time to check all Amy's files when Gabe called about the ID of the second dead person at the Pattersons'. I tried tracking the IP address of skullandcrossbones from one of the emails the person sent Amy, but it led me to an internet café in Naples, which could mean a dead end."

"So our one lead has been stolen?" He turned, closed the window and locked it, then headed for the hallway. "We need to let Gabe know about this."

As Michael and Kyra traversed to the last house on the road, he couldn't shake the feeling he should have been able to prevent this somehow. If he hadn't had to deliver the baby last night, maybe Amy wouldn't have snuck out of the house and gotten caught up in whatever was going on. The pressure behind his eyes intensified. If anything happened to his little sister, he would never be able to forgive himself.

Memories of Sarah intruded into his mind. How long had he been unconscious at the wreck? If he'd awakened sooner, could he have somehow saved her from dying? Why hadn't God helped him? Michael had pleaded with Him to give him the ability to keep Sarah alive. If only he…

He shook his head, trying to rid his thoughts of the same what-ifs he'd been going over for the past year. A doctor dealt with death—especially an emergency-room physician. He'd been contemplating resigning his position as an E.R. doctor when Ginny asked him to come back to Flamingo Cay to be Amy's guardian until she graduated from high school. The town had been without a doctor for a while and needed another one. He'd thought returning home had been an answer to his dilemma, that it would give him the time to reevaluate his life. Now he wasn't so sure. Now he'd added more emotional baggage on top of what he already carried.

Kyra approached Gabe in the Pattersons' backyard near the beach where the first victim had been found. "Someone was in Michael's house while we went to talk with Laurie. Amy's laptop is gone."

"Did you get anything off it?" Gabe chewed on a toothpick.

Kyra told him about the journal and their visit to see Laurie. "The IP address for the message from skullandcrossbones leads to a place called Kava Net in Naples."

After removing the toothpick from his mouth,

he snapped it in two and stuffed the pieces into his top shirt pocket. "We can check it out if we don't find Amy today. If it's okay with you, Michael, I'll have Nichols check the window and desk area for fingerprints."

"Sure." He unsnapped a key from his keychain and gave it to Gabe.

"Amy's kayak is still at the Main Street dock where she keeps it. Right next to yours, Michael. So your sister isn't likely in the swamp," Gabe said.

"Kyra and I are still going to check some places in the Glades. I can't shake the feeling when Amy has been upset with me or someone, she often went into it."

"Fine. I'm not gonna stop you." Gabe shifted his attention to Kyra. "I seem to remember it wasn't your favorite place to be." Amusement laced his voice.

Kyra grinned. "I seem to remember rescuing you from a wasp in your office once."

"Hey, they sting and I swell up like an overinflated ball. Let me know if you find anything."

Kyra turned to leave, paused and glanced back. "Aren't you through with the crime scene?"

"Something's been nagging me. I thought another walk-through would jiggle my mind."

"Has it?"

"Nope." Gabe ambled toward his car and slipped

behind the steering wheel. "But it'll come to me, probably in the middle of the night."

Kyra walked beside Michael as Gabe waved and drove toward the end of the block.

"I never bothered to ask, but do you have a boat? Please tell me you do, that we aren't hiking into the swamp and that the boat is bigger than a canoe or kayak."

Michael chuckled as he opened the passenger door for Kyra. "I'll borrow my partner's boat. It's an airboat, and it can cover a lot of ground."

"That's great," she said, climbing into the front. "Being several feet above the water is better than in the water. Do you know how to drive one? I seem to remember they aren't easy, and people have accidents when they don't know what they're doing."

"You would never know you grew up on the edge of a swamp, and yes, I know how to drive one." Michael turned the ignition key, backed out of the driveway and headed toward Bay Shore Drive. He thought of her aversion to snakes. He had enough guilt to carry around, first with Sarah and now Amy. He didn't need to add Kyra to his baggage. "Are you sure you want to go with me? I can do this alone."

She twisted around and captured his attention. "I'm sure. If Amy is in trouble, two people are better than one."

A vision of Amy running for her life took over his thoughts. A tremor shimmied down his length.

"I'm kinda surprised you don't have an airboat since as a kid you spent a lot of time in the swamp."

Kyra's comment lured him away from the disconcerting direction his mind was taking him. "My two-man kayak is all I need. I'm usually not in any hurry when I do get to go into the Glades. I like to park it somewhere and watch the birds and animals. An airboat scares the wildlife away."

"How often do you get to do it?"

"Not nearly enough. A lot of my older patients need special care. More than a ten- or fifteen-minute office visit allows."

The care she heard in his voice gave her a glimpse into the man Michael had grown up to be. She wanted to know more. "You enjoy working with older patients?"

He pulled up into a driveway of a large house that backed up to the main canal. "Yes. I didn't realize how much until I moved here. I saw my share in the emergency room, but managing an older patient's health on an ongoing basis is so different."

"Then it looks like you came to the right place since a lot of people retire here. What made you go into emergency medicine?"

"I liked the challenge, trying to figure out what

was wrong, often quickly, and do something about it." A terse undercurrent threaded through his voice.

Kyra studied his face, wiped of all expression as he stared straight ahead. "I imagine that can be quite hectic at times." She could identify with that. Going into a situation where a suspect might have a gun. Having to make a spur-of-the-moment decision on the person's intent. "You must still have challenges with your patients."

He dragged his gaze to hers. "Yes, and even some decisions that have to be made quickly." His features still were neutral except for a sadness in his eyes. Fleeting before he masked it. "This is Ken's house. He told me where he keeps the key to the boat out back off his dock."

"Let's go." She exited his Saturn and strolled next to him to the patio where he retrieved a key hidden in a frog.

Michael was wrestling with something beyond his sister missing. Something that happened in Chicago? Something to do with the woman he'd thought of marrying? She'd learned to read people well in her line of work, and this man beside her was struggling with a problem beyond what was going on in Flamingo Cay. The curiosity that had aided her as a police detective surfaced.

He boarded the boat first, then turned to help her. Placing her hand in his, she stepped onto the craft bobbing in the water.

Instead of immediately releasing his grasp, she squeezed his fingers gently, looking up into his eyes. "We'll find her."

A few seconds passed, their gazes bound, before Michael cupped her hand between his two. "Thank you for coming. This means a lot to me."

His attention totally directed at her cleared all words from her mind. Her attraction to him grew. She swallowed, tried to come up with something to say and settled on giving him a nod. He was Ginny's little brother. What was she thinking? She couldn't rid her mind of a nine-year-old kid hiding under his big sister's bed, listening to Ginny and Kyra talk about boys. He only got caught because of his snickers, then for weeks he kidded both of them about the guys they liked.

A fleeting half smile graced his lips. "We don't have a lot of time, but we should be able to check out her favorite haunts, at least the ones I know about."

He let go of her hand and moved toward the driver's seat. Leaving her to deal with myriad sensations rolling through her. The one that overrode all others was that her attraction to Michael Hunt had come at the worst possible time.

As the sun sank toward the horizon, the shadows crept farther out into the water. Sitting in front of Michael, Kyra hugged her arms to her. In spite of the warm, humid air, coldness embedded itself in her from the moment Michael had left the dock and grown to encompass her whole body the farther away from Flamingo Cay they had traveled.

A memory, buried for years, overwhelmed all thoughts. She remembered the sensation of falling through the air into the murky swamp. The sound of the splash as she hit it. The frantic flapping of her arms tangled in the lily pads on the surface of the stream. The dirty taste of the briny water. Her father's shouts to move fast. A large snake—later identified as a water moccasin—headed straight for her. She hadn't recalled that until she saw a snake slither across the canal and disappear among the overhanging branches of the mangrove island nearby.

After an unsuccessful search, Michael directed the boat back into the main canal that led to town. A scowl etched deep lines into his tan face. Over the noise from the huge fan, he shouted, "I don't know of any other places to look. She hasn't said much lately about where she likes to go in the swamp."

"At least we've ruled out those areas. Gabe's probably right. She isn't in the swamp." What person in their right mind would be? Kyra scanned the growing darkness and quaked.

"We're almost back to Ken's." Michael steered the airboat around a sharp bend.

Houses came into view, and Kyra began to relax some. But the coldness still clung to her. She'd come back to Flamingo Cay to lie on the beach, soak up some sun and relax. Not go into a place that created nightmares in her mind.

Gabe strode across the yard toward the pier as Michael pulled up to it and tossed the rope to Kyra to tie the boat to the mooring. When she finished, she rotated toward the police chief covering the short length of wooden planks to the end.

"What's up?" she asked, realizing by the steely glint in Gabe's eyes and the rigid set of his shoulders that this wasn't a social call.

Michael hopped off the boat. "We didn't find anything. How about you?"

Gabe blew out a long breath. "Wilson just got a location on Amy's cell, and you ain't gonna like it. Smack-dab in the middle of Alligator Island."

FIVE

Two large, battery-powered spotlights Gabe carried in his patrol car illuminated the path to Alligator Island, revealing the coffee-colored water of the narrow canal off the main one. The sound of the airboat announced their approach and Kyra hoped alerted all the alligators in the area to flee. An occasional sight in the dark of red eyes lurking above the water reminded her of her casual comment to Michael earlier about not being afraid of alligators. She wasn't. She had no reason to be, but that didn't mean she didn't have a healthy respect for them and a desire to keep her distance.

"We're here," Gabe announced from the front of the boat as Michael guided the craft up onto solid ground. "I don't know why I let you talk me into coming, Michael. I don't think we can do a thorough search in the dark."

Michael cut the engine and lifted up a powerful flashlight. "This will help. I would have come with or without you. If there's a chance I can find

Amy tonight, I'm taking it. A lot can happen before morning comes."

"I just want you to know the chances are slim we'll find anything." Gabe swept his arm wide. "There are a lot of places to hide in the trees. Too dense for us to penetrate tonight." Grimacing, the police chief held up his flashlight. "Even with these."

After grabbing hers, Kyra followed Michael and Gabe onto the island. Her only other pair of tennis shoes sank into the muddy ground near the canal. "Should we spread out? Go in different directions?"

"Normally I would say yes but it's not wise in the dark. Let's keep a visual sight on each other so if anything happens there's help. Kyra, you've got your gun so you take one side. Michael, you'll be in the middle, and I'll be on the other side."

The farther apart Kyra went from Michael, the more goose bumps rose on her skin even though the temperature was near ninety degrees and the humidity was one hundred percent. At least it felt as if it was. Her damp shirt clung to her, and sweat and dust caked her face. Her heart raced, and her lungs burned from lack of enough oxygen.

Sweeping her flashlight in a wide arc, she searched for anything that would indicate Amy was on the island. If she could find Amy, then she could leave.

Odors assaulted her nostrils, smells of cinnamon from the mangrove trees mingling with the aroma of the pines, the decaying vegetation inches thick in places, the earthiness of the muddy ground and the saltiness from where the Gulf mixed with the fresh water of the swamp. She'd grown up with these odors but had forgotten how powerful they were. They brought back memories of her childhood when she did venture out into the marsh before she'd allowed fear to keep her away. Since that encounter with the water moccasin, she had faced so many dangerous situations and had walked away fine. So why was she letting a childhood fear cause her heart to beat faster and her hands to shake?

"Amy, Amy," Michael called out.

A bellow echoed through the Glades in answer. Taken by surprise, Kyra gasped, her heartbeat kicking up another notch. Until she realized it was a male alligator. Thankfully, he sounded far away. At least she thought so. She paused, fingering her gun in her holster.

"That's probably ole Jaws," Gabe shouted with a hint of amusement in his voice.

"You mean he's still alive?" Kyra remembered the stories about him from when she lived here. At that time, he was at least ten feet long, and people estimated he was old then, a product of the alligator farm that had been on the island for a short time in the early eighties. He'd managed to escape right before the place went under, and he'd ruled the area.

"Yup. People sight him from time to time. Probably sixteen feet by now. Scared some tourists a few months back. They hightailed it out of here so fast they were a blur. But don't worry. From what I've heard and seen he stays away from here. Bad memories of his childhood possibly."

The chuckle in Gabe's voice made her frown. She started to answer him but decided ignoring him would be the best. But the words tumbled out of her mouth before she could stop them. "Anyone in their right mind would not want to encounter a sixteen-foot alligator, including you, unless you're off your rocker."

Gabe laughed. "Touché. If it will make you feel better, when I heard him, I jumped."

Listening to her mentor teasing her caused the tension to slip away. It was time she faced her fear and overcame it. But if she had to, she preferred doing that in the light of day.

Michael stopped walking and turned in a circle, shouting, "Amy, if you're out here, show yourself. I'm here to help." He waited a half minute, then added, "Please, Amy, come out."

Only silence greeted his plea. Kyra wanted to comfort him. His pain, reflected in his voice, cloaked his face. "We'll find her," she said, hoping that was the truth.

He looked at her for a long moment, then swung around and began his hike forward again.

But she'd seen the doubt in his eyes. The longer it took them to find Amy, the less the possibility of finding her alive.

When they were halfway across the small island, Michael's flashlight stopped on a spot a little in front of him. Then suddenly he started running toward the area. "I think I found the cell."

As Michael bent down to pick up the phone, Kyra sloshed through the mud toward him. A few yards away from him, she sank to above her ankles in the boggy ground. Another step and she was in up to the middle of her calves. With each movement forward it became more difficult, zapping her strength. Shining her light around her, she noticed the muddy earth went on for a couple more feet but where Michael was the ground was higher.

Gabe joined Michael and took the cell. "Is this Amy's?"

"Yes." Michael yelled his sister's name above the racket the insects made. "What if she is unconscious or something? What if the killer found her cell and put it here? Or what if she lost it here?"

"Remember, Amy said the killer had her cell. How did she know he did?" Kyra asked as she labored to cover the distance to the men. "We really don't know what happened. Amy might not, either. She was scared and getting ready to run when she left that email."

"I'm familiar with this island, and there isn't any kind of cabin left on it. The last hurricane took down the remaining structure from the alligator farm. So I don't think this is where Amy lost her phone." Gabe took off his ball cap and scratched his head. "Which might mean the killer had it and left it here so we would find it. Why?"

"I don't know. I have a hard time thinking like a murderer." Michael swung his flashlight toward Kyra. "Are you all right?" He started toward her.

"I'm okay. Stay there. There's no reason for both of us to be stuck in the mud. Good thing there's no quicksand in the Everglades or I'd be worried right now."

"You mean you didn't believe those tales I told you about the quicksand?"

Kyra chuckled. "Gabe, Dad informed me after you left that evening that you embellished on the truth. It might make for a good scene in a movie, but in real life people don't go under in quicksand."

"Who, me? Embellish?"

"I'm not even going to reply to that. I know how much you liked to tease me when I was growing up. Still do." Kyra trudged a few more paces, sweat pouring off her face. Finally she reached more stable ground, and Michael clasped her hand, drawing her toward him. "We definitely need to avoid that area." She glanced down at the murk that covered her from the knees down. "I'm going to have to buy a new pair of tennis shoes. Ruined two in one day. A record for me."

"Nah. Those will wash right up. They'll be maybe a little worn from this but wearable." Gabe turned toward the way they came. "We found what we came for. I'll come back tomorrow morning to look around. I don't want to disturb any more of this ground than we already have. I might be able to discover a trail."

"But what if Amy is here?" Michael stood still.

"She isn't, and there is no cabin on this island. It might rain tonight. Amy's a smart girl and would want to find some kind of shelter if possible." Gabe plopped his ball cap back on his head and continued toward the boat.

"Amy might have little choice in where to hide. I'm finishing what we came to do. Check this place out. I'll skirt this area, but I'm continuing on." Michael backtracked a few yards and then circumvented where the cell had been discovered.

Kyra trailed after him. No way would she let him go alone.

Gabe huffed behind them and came after them. "If you see footprints, avoid them."

They returned to the airboat thirty minutes later. Kyra walked out into the canal a few feet to rinse off the worst of the mud from her legs. The mosquitoes had feasted on what skin was exposed to them. Rubbing a bite on her arm, she clamored into the craft.

On the way back to the airboat, Michael had remained silent while Gabe did a running commentary on the demise of the alligator farm. He'd been a young man at the time and had frequently visited the place before it went under due to lack of visitors. Off the beaten track, Flamingo Cay wasn't a tourist attraction.

"I'm sorry we didn't find Amy, Michael. It was a long shot," Gabe said when he came on board.

"But at least we ruled out her being on Alligator Island." Michael switched on the engine and headed back toward his partner's dock on the main canal.

Wet from her mini bath in the water, Kyra hugged her arms to herself and shivered from the wind created by the fast speed the craft was going. She thought of her safe, dry house in Dallas and knew she would appreciate it even more when she got home. When she saw the lights of the pier come into view, she sagged back in her seat in relief. At least the breeze had dried off most of the water by the time she hopped onto the dock.

"I'll check the island again tomorrow. Like I said, I want to see if I can pick up a trail. I'll see if Harvey and Boomer can join me." Gabe took the lights he supplied for the journey and made his way across the back of Ken's property.

"I want to be in on it." Michael stopped at the frog near the patio and put the keys back since the house was dark.

"No, the fewer people who go, the faster I can cover the island and the less any evidence will be disturbed. The only reason we went tonight was in case Amy was there with her phone. She wasn't. Now you let me handle it from here."

"I'd like to check out Kava Net in Naples tomorrow morning, if that's okay with you, Gabe." Kyra placed her hand on the door handle of Michael's Saturn.

"That would be great. The sheriff is helping me to organize a search of the swamp and land around Flamingo Cay. We should be ready to start that by ten."

"You'll be back from Alligator Island by then?" Michael punched his key button to open the doors.

"Yes, I'm going out when the sun comes up. I'll call you if we find anything. Otherwise meet me at the public pier tomorrow at ten. We'll start our search from then." Gabe climbed into his patrol car as they got into the Saturn.

Michael waited until Gabe pulled out before he turned on his vehicle, then slanted toward Kyra. "I need to help find Amy. Can you talk Gabe into letting us or at least me go tomorrow?"

"Let Gabe do his job. He's a great tracker. I'm not. Are you?"

"No."

"I think we need to check out this skullandcross-bones lead at the Kava Net. If we can take as many pictures of Amy's friends as possible, it might help us rule some of them out as the mysterious email friend."

"She loves to take pictures and has a nice digital camera I gave her for Christmas. I know she has taken photos with it when she goes into the swamp. I didn't think about that. There may be something on the camera to help tomorrow in the search."

"Maybe, and if we can get snapshots of her friends that should help, too."

He backed out of the driveway and drove toward Pelican Lane. "It should be somewhere in her room."

"We can look together and come up with what we need. Most coffee places open early. I can call and find out when, and we can be there when they open the doors in the morning."

He threw her a lopsided grin. "Sounds like a plan. At least I'll feel like I'm doing something."

"I'll run home and take a quick shower and change, then be back at your house to help you. It wouldn't hurt to go completely through Amy's room and see if we find anything that might help."

"I'll come in. I haven't had a chance to see how

your aunt is doing. She must be upset by what happened today next door."

"I know she would love to see you, but I was informed earlier that she could take care of herself. Did you know she beat Gabe at a shooting contest?"

"I heard rumors of that."

"And she has a gun she's been carrying around all day."

"Like her niece."

As a police officer for so many years, wearing a weapon had become so second nature to her that she rarely even thought about it now.

When they entered Kyra's childhood home, Aunt Ellen came out into the hallway from the kitchen. Her smile grew when she laid eyes on Michael.

Petite, only coming to Michael's shoulders, her aunt approached him and wrapped her arms around him, hugging him. "I'm so sorry to hear about Amy. I'm glad you're here. I baked you some cookies and was thinking about coming down to your house with them. Now you've saved me a trip, young man. Come on into the kitchen while I put them in a container for you." She retraced her steps.

Kyra placed her hand on Michael's arm as he started after Aunt Ellen. "A word of caution. She's a dear but not a very good cook. One time she made me some cookies and sent them to me. I think she put salt in instead of sugar. Another time they weren't cooked completely. So you might wait to try one in the privacy of your house."

He grinned. "I've already received her gifts before. She'll never know."

Kyra passed the doorway into the kitchen as Michael went inside and heard Aunt Ellen saying, "I wish I'd known y'all were coming. I could have waited dinner. Do you want me to whip together something for you and Kyra?"

"That's all right," Michael answered immediately. "It's been taken care of. Kyra is changing and then we're going to my house to try and figure out where Amy is."

Smooth. Kyra chuckled and hurried to her bedroom.

Michael sat on Amy's rumpled covers on her bed. "We still haven't found her digital camera."

Kyra stood in the middle of the room, making a slow circle. "Where does she usually keep it?"

He shrugged. "Amy made it clear from the beginning her bedroom was her domain. Most of the time her door is closed. The couple of times it's been open I only saw her camera on her dresser once. Usually I see it when she's leaving to go take pictures. I know it's important to her because she has expressed an interest in pursuing photography.

Do you think the person who took her laptop took her camera, too?"

Again Kyra scanned the area, trying to figure out where Amy would have put it. They had already gone through her drawers and closet. There wasn't any obvious place left and their exploration had come up empty of anything else that might help them. "Do you think she had her camera with her yesterday in the swamp?"

"I was at work. I don't know. And that seems to be the problem. I don't know what's really going on with Amy. So I can't help her." Michael curled his fingers into fists on the bedding beside him.

"Is there somewhere else in the house she might have set the camera down?"

Tilting his head to the side, he stared at the doorway into the hall. When his eyes brightened, he swiveled his attention toward her. "Maybe. A couple of times I've seen it in the den. Once in the kitchen. Usually that's right after she comes back into the house. She'd grab something to eat and put it down."

"Then we should search the whole place to make sure." Kyra made her way into the hallway. "The other thing we need to consider is that she lost her camera along with her cell."

"But she didn't mention that in her email."

"Because she was letting skullandcrossbones know that she doesn't have her cell with her if that person wanted to call. If we don't find out anything at Kava Net tomorrow morning, maybe if we find the camera, the pictures on it will help me."

"If it's here." Michael went into the kitchen.

When they came up empty in that room, they moved to the den. Kyra checked around the couch and bookcase while Michael examined the rest of the area.

"It's not here." Disappointment tugged his mouth into a frown.

"Where else did she hang out when home?"

"Her bathroom. She rarely went into my bedroom or formal living and dining room. The same with the spare bedroom."

"Okay. Let's check out her bathroom. I can remember spending hours in mine as a teenager."

In the long hallway he gestured toward the end. "That's hers. Thankfully we have a guest bathroom, because the last time I glanced inside Amy's I would have declared it a disaster zone. Housekeeping isn't one of her strong suits. Mine neither."

Kyra strode down the hall. "I've got news for you. I hate housework. That's why I hired a lady to come in once a week. Best money I spent on myself."

"I was going to do that. Just haven't found the time to go through the whole hiring process."

Kyra opened the door then peered over her shoulder at Michael. "I'd move that to the top of your to-do list. You weren't kidding when you said this room was a disaster."

He looked around her. "It's worse than I remember. Maybe the person who took her laptop tossed this room."

"Nope. It doesn't have that feel." Kyra's gaze skimmed over the towels on the floor under the wall rack, then over the makeup covering the counter, some bottles left open, blue powder littering the beige top. Behind a blow-dryer lying on its side, she saw a camera. "I found it."

"Great." Michael took it from Kyra and started down the hall. "And when this is over with, I'm finding a maid."

In the den he took a seat on the couch and turned on the camera to search the stored pictures. Clicking through the photos still left on the memory card, Michael shook his head. "None of her friends, and I don't recognize this place."

"Looks like a cabin or should I say an abandoned cabin." Kyra leaned close to Michael to get a better look at the pic. "This might not have been taken at the same place as the others. Do you know where there's an abandoned cabin?"

"I couldn't say. There were some when I was growing up, but with the hurricanes that have blown through the Glades, those may be gone. That's something we need to show Gabe. He might know. Do you think this place has anything to do with her disappearance?"

"The cabin shot and the two following it are time-stamped yesterday, so yes, it could have. This last one is too fuzzy. Is that two men by the line of trees?"

Michael examined the digital-camera screen. "I don't know. It looks like she took it while moving fast." The color faded from his face. "What if she was running away from the bad guy?"

"This was taken in the early afternoon. Why didn't she say something to you if she thought the guy was bad and chasing her? Let's see if Gabe can ID the place. I'll give him a call and have him come over."

"While you do that, I'll put the memory card into my printer and run off all the pictures. If he can identify them, we have somewhere to start tomorrow in the search of the surrounding swamp."

Her stomach rumbling, Kyra rose and walked toward the kitchen and the half-eaten pizza they hadn't finished over an hour ago. She loved cold pizza about as much as a hot one, and with all that had happened today, she hadn't eaten much.

She picked up the box to take back into the den when Gabe's voice came on the phone. "Can you come by Michael's? We found some pictures on Amy's camera of a place in the swamp that she went yesterday. Michael doesn't know where it is. Maybe you'll be able to tell."

"I was heading home. I'll be there in ten minutes."

When Michael reentered the den, his gaze seized hers from across the room. For a minute he didn't say anything before breaking the visual tether and glancing down at what he held. "Still can't tell much about the places these were taken. I did remember Amy threw away her yearbook a couple of days ago in my office trash can."

"Why?" she managed to get out while her pulse reacted to the brief electric moment between them. All she could think about was how different Michael was from the teenager she'd known sixteen years ago but at the same time familiar, as though they had been together for those years.

"They're mailed in August to the students who bought one. She was upset by her picture in it. She couldn't believe she had listened to Ginny and had her photo taken looking like—" he flipped through the yearbook and showed her Amy "—a normal teen. That's my assessment, not hers."

"I can see both you and Ginny in her, especially without the heavy black eyeliner and mascara."

"Not to mention her unusually pale skin and out-of-the-bottle black hair."

"If she spends so much time outdoors, how is she so pale?"

"Lots of sunscreen and she stays in the shade where she can or wears a hat to keep her face that way. I should be thrilled she doesn't like to roast her skin to a dark tan like her contemporaries."

"Why the gothic look?"

"I don't know. I think it started when Ginny got ready to go to the Philippines."

"That could explain a lot. In her mind she's lost her mother and now Ginny. Even though Ginny wanted Amy to go with her, Amy feels abandoned by her, too."

"And then I came back to Flamingo Cay and buried myself in my work. Not reassuring for a girl who is feeling that way."

"Do you want to talk about it?" Would he say anything to her about what was really going on his life? For some reason she wanted to know—to help him.

"Talking about it won't change the fact I let my sister down. For that matter both of my sisters."

His voice, expression and stance screamed a need to unload a burden. "No, it won't change what has happened, but maybe talking will help you."

His laugh was humorless. "I don't think anything will help at the moment."

She turned away, disappointed that she was being shut out and bothered she felt that way. The doorbell rang. "That's probably Gabe."

"I'll get it." Michael put the yearbook and photos down on the coffee table.

As he headed for the front door, she said, "Check the peephole, though, just to make sure," then winced when she stated what should be obvious in the type of situation they were in.

The sound of Gabe's voice coming from the foyer released her pent-up breath. She shifted toward the men coming back into the room.

She gave Gabe a grin. "Have you had a chance to eat dinner yet?"

"Dinner? What's that?" Gabe slid a glance to Michael standing by the threshold into the den, then to Kyra.

She ignored the wealth of questions lurking in the perceptive depth of her mentor's eyes and lifted up her slice of Canadian-bacon-and-extra-cheese. "We have some leftover cold pizza if you want any."

Gabe scrunched up his face into a look of loathing. "How can you eat that cold?"

"Easy." Kyra took a bite while Michael finally came farther into the room, his features now reflecting a bland expression.

He picked up the pictures from the camera and passed them to the police chief. "None of these look familiar, but places could have changed since I lived here."

Gabe shuffled through the stack, noting the time stamped on the photos. "The first ones were along Crystal Clear Creek. I'm not sure about the last three. We don't have any abandoned cabins near Flamingo Cay."

Michael's forehead creased, his eyes narrowing. "So Amy could have gone a ways from town?"

"If she took them, yes. But just to make sure, I'll show these pictures to a few men who spend more time in the Glades than I do."

"As far as I know she wouldn't let anyone use her camera." Michael came to Kyra's side and scooped up a piece of pizza.

"I think if we can identify where she took those last three we might be one step closer to finding her. Something happened yesterday that put what happened this morning in motion."

"We don't know that, Kyra." Gabe snatched up a slice of pizza and grimaced as he took a bite then walked to the trash can and dropped it in.

"Call it women's intuition if you want."

Gabe chuckled. "Don't pull that on me."

"Whatever it is, I've learned to listen to it. I know for a fact you've had gut instincts before and gone with them."

One of the police chief's eyebrows rose. "Is that what you discovered when you were eavesdropping on me and your dad?"

"I should have figured you knew I was."

"Kinda hard not to. You weren't very subtle back then."

"I've gained a few skills in that area."

"Good to know."

"Did you track down Kip Thomas at the address I found attached to the skullandcrossbones email?" Kyra savored her pizza, realizing how little she'd eaten that day.

"I haven't heard back from my inquiry yet, but I'll give the chief in Naples a call tomorrow to see. Are you still going to Kava Net in the morning?"

"Yes. If I can get a photo of who it is from a security camera, that could help us. We're taking a yearbook and asking about various people Amy knows. Maybe someone will recognize a person from the yearbook and link them to Amy. I know this is a long shot, but I still think we need to check out this email connection. Amy sent a parting message to this person."

"We could use a break. I'll let myself out. Y'all go on and enjoy that." Gabe's mouth pinched up into an expression that reminded Kyra of when she'd taken an awful-tasting medicine as a child. He touched the cap of his ball hat, then sauntered toward the foyer.

Not a word was said until the sound of the front door shutting reached Kyra and Michael. Then they burst out laughing.

"I get the impression he isn't a fan of cold pizza," Kyra said, then popped the last bite into her mouth and enjoyed it.

"I learned to appreciate it when I was working long shifts in the E.R. and had to come back to finish my dinner."

"I feel better now that we have a yearbook and Gabe is looking into those pictures.

"A couple of his officers spend a lot of time in the Glades on their off hours. Maybe one of them will know. Tomorrow's going to be a long day. I'd better head home." Kyra crossed toward the French doors that led out onto the deck in the back, facing the Gulf. "About all we can do now is pray we find something useful tomorrow."

"You think that's going to do any good?"

Kyra stopped and swung back toward Michael. "Yes, as a matter of fact, I do."

He snorted and busied himself with picking up the almost empty pizza box. "I used to think that but now I'm not so sure."

"Praying lets the Lord know what you need or want."

He glared at her. "Right now it's not looking too good for Amy. She's out there in the dark somewhere, scared, not sure where to go for help."

"Whether you do or not, I'll be praying for Amy's safe return. That's something I can do.

Good night. I'll see you tomorrow at seven so we can get to Kava Net by eight."

She exited the house and crossed his back deck toward the beach. The moonlight streamed across the relatively calm Gulf. With a gentle breeze blowing to cool a still-hot night, Kyra trudged along the shore. Halfway to her home she paused, removed her shoes and turned toward the water, listening to the small waves break against the shore. Their rhythmic sound lulled her into a sense of peace after a horrific day. The feel of sand between her toes felt reassuring, bringing with it memories of how she'd loved to play on the beach for hours as a child.

She closed her eyes and let the soothing caress of the night envelop her. *Lord, please bring Amy back safely to Michael. Help them to mend their differences. Help Michael to find peace and—*

From behind, a muscled arm locked around her neck, slamming her back against a hard chest as her assailant drew the gun at her waist.

SIX

Michael stared at the French doors that Kyra disappeared through. Her words about praying for Amy rang in his ears. He used to pray all the time. But since the wreck with Sarah, he'd slowly given it up as he wrestled with his faith. Finding excuses not to stop and pray when there was a need.

He should be doing everything he could to get Amy back safely—including praying to God. Michael made his way outside onto the deck, the sound of the Gulf in the distance, a calming sound that reached into his soul to soothe.

Lord, it's been a long time. I'm not sure where to even begin. Even if You are angry with me, please help Amy. Even if... Words flowing through his mind came to a halt. Nothing formed in his thoughts. Blank.

Was that the Lord's answer?

He focused on the night around him—the waves crashing against the shore, an owl hooting, the fragrance from the jasmine near the deck.

Drawn toward the beach, Michael descended the steps to the deck and headed toward the stretch of sand and sea.

For a second, Kyra's attacker shifted his arm, relieving the choking pressure around her neck. Instantly she sagged, using the dead weight of her body to slip through the steel cage of her assailant's embrace. As she sank toward the sand, she twisted about and kicked him several times. The Glock went flying across the beach. He groaned and doubled over. She backpedaled away from the man in black toward where her weapon landed. Quickly he recovered from the strategically placed hits and withdrew a knife from a sheath at his side, its blade glittering in the ray of moonlight slanting through the tree branches. He crouched to pounce on her.

In the dark shadows of the palm trees, she felt around for her Glock. Nothing but sand. She balled a hand around a fistful of grains and threw it into his face. Most of them ended up caught in the fabric of his ski mask. She couldn't tell if any landed in his eyes until he staggered back a few paces, bringing his free hand up to brush at his face. Which gave her time to scramble to her feet.

She dug her toes into the sand. Suddenly her assailant exploded forward, rushing her with the knife, aiming for her heart. She lunged to the right.

So did her attacker, taking her down to the beach. She clasped the wrist of the hand that held the knife, squeezing as hard as she could while his crushing weight pinned her down.

He struck her across the cheek, a ring or something cutting into her flesh. The force of the punch caused her ears to ring and his black-clad hulk to waver before her eyes. Still she didn't take her gaze off the knife hovering inches from her chest. Adrenaline pumped through her but so did exhaustion from the long day.

He hit her again in the jaw.

Her mind went hazy. Her vision blurred. Her hand gripping the attacker's wrist shook.

The knife crept even nearer.

Michael glanced in the direction of Kyra's house. He should go see her before she went to bed. Apologize for how the evening ended. He took a step toward that direction and halted. The tired circles beneath her eyes had emphasized how exhausted she was. He could tell her tomorrow and not disturb her tonight.

He started to turn toward his deck when a flash caught his eyes a couple of houses down from his. He stopped and squinted into the darkness. Two lovers on the beach?

Then he saw a hand lift up, hang in the air for a

second then come crashing down into the face of the person on the bottom. Michael took off running toward the pair.

As the assailant trapped Kyra against the sand, the pressure on her body made each breath she inhaled difficult—precious. Sweat drenched her as Kyra struggled for control of the knife, for a decent gulp of air. From deep inside her, she drew on a well of strength. With everything she had left, she twisted and bucked, trying to dislodge her attacker. She pummeled his back with a fist.

He shifted off her chest and stomach to capture her fist hitting him. The movement allowed oxygen-rich air to flood her lungs. She screamed, a piercing sound that she hoped curdled his blood.

The sound of the cry for help spurred Michael faster. As he grew closer, rays from the moon washed over the pair on the ground. A man in black and a woman. Kyra.

Rage fueled Michael the remaining few yards. A screeching noise, like a long-ago warrior, came from him.

The assailant on top of Kyra jerked his attention toward Michael.

Suddenly the attacker leaped to his feet and raced in the opposite direction.

Michael slowed by Kyra. "Are you okay?"

"Yes."

That was all he needed. He increased his pace, intending to go after the man in black.

"Don't, Michael," Kyra shouted out. "He's armed."

Decreasing his pace to a jog, he peered over his shoulder, saw her pushing up onto her knees and trying to stand. She went down. He swung around and headed back to Kyra. She wasn't all right.

Seconds later he was at her side, helping her to her feet. "Why didn't you tell me you're hurt?"

"I'm fine."

"No, you're not. You're shaking." She turned her face toward him, moonlight bathing her face. "You're bleeding."

"It's nothing." On her feet, Kyra swayed toward him, her chest rising and falling rapidly. "My gun. Over there."

He peered in the direction she pointed but didn't see it.

She stepped toward it and wobbled.

"Take it easy. I'll look for it." Under the trees he patted the sandy beach until he encountered the barrel of the Glock. "Got it."

"He grabbed me and the gun before I knew what hit me."

The quaver in her voice aroused his anger all over. All he wanted to do was go after her attacker—pound his fists into his face for what the man had done to Kyra. His arm went around her and supported some of her weight as he moved toward his house. "I want to make sure you're okay. Clean those cuts."

"Really, I've had worse."

He looked into her face, the light from his deck showcasing the blood streaming down her cheeks. His heart constricted at the sight of her injuries. Thankfully the cuts didn't appear deep enough to need stitches. But he wouldn't be sure until he got inside his house and really examined them.

Pushing the door open, he let her go first into the den, but he quickly followed. She wanted to act as though nothing was wrong. He knew differently. The ashen cast to her features attested to that fact.

"Have a seat. I'll go get my bag."

Kyra watched Michael leave the den and eased down onto the couch. Aches and pain began to demand her attention. She was afraid to even look at her face.

She dug into her shorts pocket and pulled out her cell. Gabe answered on the second ring.

"I hate to bother you again tonight—"

The chief's chuckle floated to her. "You're not."

Her throat tight, she swallowed hard. "Gabe, I was attacked on my way back to my house this evening."

"When? Where?" All humor fled his voice.

"About five minutes ago. On the beach between my house and Michael's. The man was dressed in black—including a ski mask. He had a knife. He was about five feet maybe nine or ten inches, medium built. It was hard to tell exactly since he came up behind me, then everything happened fast. I'm not sure it's the same man as the killer. Maybe it's the man who went with the second set of footprints found near the scene of the murders."

"Are you all right?"

"Yes, I'll be fine. It's takes more than a wrestling match to get me down."

"How bad off is the other guy?" A chuckle came back into his voice.

"I got a few well-placed kicks in. He'll be hurting for a while."

"Do you remember anything else?"

She closed her eyes and tried to remember the scuffle. Her mind drew a blank. She lifted a trembling hand and hooked the stray strands of hair pulled from her ponytail behind her ears. "No, I wish I did."

"Where are you now?"

"Michael's, but you don't need to come over. The man took off fast toward the Pattersons'. I'm sure he's long gone by now."

"That's okay. I'm still coming to look around."

She returned her cell to her pocket as Michael reentered the den. "I let Gabe know what happened."

"And he's coming over."

"How did you guess?"

Michael sat beside her on the couch and opened his black bag. "Because that's Gabe, and I can tell how much he cares about you."

"This town is blessed to have had someone like him as police chief for over twenty years."

"I know he thinks Wilson is a good replacement for him and I'm sure he will be, but there will be a lot of people who'll miss Gabe."

"You make it sound like he'll move away from Flamingo Cay."

"Believe it or not, I think he might. He's been talking about going up north to retire."

"Up north? Most people come to Florida to retire."

"That's our chief. Never like the crowd. He said something about his son up north and being near him and his family." Michael dabbed a cold wet cotton ball on her cuts.

Kyra winced from the sting of the antiseptic solution. "Will I survive?"

"No thanks to that guy who attacked you. What if I hadn't come along?"

"I had things under control."

"Sure. You looked like you did."

She'd been taken off guard. She hadn't thought of herself as a target. She wouldn't make that mistake again. "What was that you were yelling?"

"Some war cry I heard in a movie. It was supposed to scare the enemy and mess with their minds."

"Well, I guess it did that. He took one look at you and ran." Kyra forced lightness into her voice, hoping to coax a smile out of Michael, whose face was set in a scowl. "I'm surprised the neighbors didn't come out to investigate."

"The couple who live in the house you were behind are hard of hearing. The husband wears a hearing aid, and I think he turns it off a lot of the time because his wife talks real loud because of her hearing problem. She refuses to acknowledge she has one." Michael put a small bandage on each cut—one by her jawline and the other right under her eye on her left cheek. "There. That should keep you awhile."

At the sound of the doorbell Michael stiffened then relaxed as he stood. "That'll be Gabe checking up on you." He took a step and peered back. "But I'll check the peephole to make sure."

The last of her adrenaline drained away, and she slumped back on the cushion and rested her head against it. She tried to rally when she heard Gabe and Michael talking near the entryway into the den. She remained where she was, listening to Gabe quiz Michael about what he saw.

The two men entered the den and locked gazes with her. The urge to squirm under both of their intense looks was strong. She squashed it and shoved herself forward.

"Okay, let's have it."

"A knife! Where was your gun?"

"He managed to get it, but I kicked it out of his hand. I just couldn't get to it."

"I want to see where it happened. This should help." Gabe hefted his powerful heavy-duty flashlight.

"You can stay here. I can show him." Michael walked toward the French doors.

"No, I'm coming, too." Kyra infused a no-nonsense attitude into her tone. "Maybe it can help me remember exactly what happened." Something niggled in the back of her mind. Something important.

Gabe waved toward her face. "Did he cut you with the knife?"

"No. When he hit me. I think it was a ring."

"A big one?"

"I can't remember. It happened so fast, and I was trying to stay focused on the hand with the knife in it."

"What did the knife look like?"

A picture flashed into her thoughts. Moon rays and the security lights the neighbors had in their backyards gave her enough illumination to remember some details of the knife. "Close to a foot long with a steel blade of five or six inches and a black handle. An expensive knife. Durable."

"Good. You're already remembering things you couldn't tell me a while back. Which hand did he hold it in?"

"Right."

Michael led the way to the spot at the back edge of the hearing-impaired couple's yard where it met the beach. A cluster of palm trees hid most of the moon from sight now.

Kyra pointed toward some large honeysuckle bushes in the couple's yard. "He was probably hiding behind there. I scanned the area as I walked, and I didn't see him. I stopped to listen to the ocean and enjoy the salty breeze. Brought back some nice memories. That's when he came up behind me and tried to lock his arms around me. I immediately started fighting, which I think threw him for a few seconds. I managed to twist away and get a few good kicks in before he launched himself at me."

"When I came running, the man fled. I should have walked her home." Michael's gaze fixed on her, scorching in its intensity.

"What if he had attacked you on the way back

to your house? We don't know if you're safe." Kyra met Michael's look with her own keen perusal.

"I can take care of myself."

"You're a doctor, not a fighter."

"You're a wo—" Michael snapped his mouth closed.

"A woman? Nice that you noticed. But this woman can take care of herself. I was managing before you came."

Gabe stepped between them, holding up his palms to each one. "That's enough, y'all. He could have gotten a drop on anyone. And everyone needs help from time to time whether it's with this case or fighting off an assailant."

The police chief's pointed stare directed at both of them eased the tension in Kyra. Michael relaxed the rigid set of his shoulders.

"This incident has changed things. But I don't have enough manpower to guard you two." Gabe withdrew a toothpick from his pocket and stuck it in his mouth.

"I'll be fine," Michael said.

"That might not be enough." Gabe chewed on his toothpick and walked toward the water, leaving them alone.

Kyra moved to Michael. "We'll protect each other."

"How do you propose we do that?"

"I run a bodyguard business. I was a cop for twelve years. I've done my share of protecting people."

"But I haven't."

"I thought you said you can take care of yourself."

Michael kneaded his nape and looked toward Gabe. "Well, I can, but I don't know about being responsible for you."

Something in the tone of his voice tugged at Kyra. "Two is more effective than one. An attacker will think twice before coming after both of us."

"Strength in numbers?"

"Exactly. You can stay with Aunt Ellen and me. Our house has a good alarm system, and besides, my aunt is packing, too." She flashed him a grin. "Two gun-toting women probably can do the job."

"Just so long as you and Ellen don't point a gun at me."

"Then it's settled. You'll stay at my house while we look for Amy. Aunt Ellen will be thrilled."

"What if Amy comes home? I need to be there. Or what if she calls the home phone?"

"You can forward your calls to my house. We can check out the house every day and leave a note if it makes you feel better, but seriously, I don't think she'll come home until we figure out what's going on or find her. I've dealt with scared people before. She's in flight mode."

Gabe sauntered back to them, sticking his chewed toothpick back in his pocket. "Have you figured out yet that you need to stay together until we solve this?"

Kyra laughed. "Yeah, we'll be staying with Aunt Ellen. I feel better about having her there. I understand she's the best shot in these here parts."

In the glow of the flashlight Gabe turned a vivid shade of red. "We'll see about that this year at the Founder's Day celebration." He checked the area one more time. "I don't see anything here, but first light tomorrow I'll be out here looking." He trudged back toward Michael's. "If we don't get this case solved soon, the townspeople aren't gonna let me retire this year."

Back inside Michael's den, Gabe said his goodbyes while Michael went to his bedroom to throw some clothes in a bag. Kyra stood at the front door, observing Gabe get into his patrol car. As he disappeared down the street, Kyra panned the area, her gaze stopping at the line of trees and thick underbrush at the end of the block.

The sensation of being watched coiled through her like a snake through the branches of the mangrove. Gripping her. Choking her. She stepped back into the house and went into the living room. Fingering the slats of the blinds apart enough to peek out, she probed the dark depths of the edge of the swamp for any sign of her attacker. He was out there using the cloak of night to hide. She could feel him.

In her bedroom, which faced the Pattersons' house and the swamp, after only four hours of fretful sleep, Kyra positioned herself at the window in the dark and peered out a small slit in the curtains. She couldn't shake the earlier feeling of someone out there watching their every move. Why? Were they getting close to something? Did the killer think she saw his face? Or was the person waiting for Amy to come home?

She didn't think the girl would, but what if she was wrong? Maybe she should rethink this and stay at Michael's. If so, somehow she needed to convince Aunt Ellen to come, too. With all that had happened, she had no doubt if the assailant thought using Aunt Ellen to get to her was necessary, he would.

She'd been in Flamingo Cay thirty hours, and she was more tired now than when she arrived for her vacation. Glancing at her bed, she thought of trying to sleep some more but knew from past experiences she wouldn't be able to. Her mind whirled with thoughts concerning the case.

With thoughts of Michael. Despite the short length of their reacquanitance, she felt bound to him—even beyond their search for Amy. They were protecting each other. He touched a place in her heart she'd thought was unreachable. Being with Michael brought back sweet memories of her childhood when she'd taken the time to play, laugh and have fun. For years, her life in Dallas had revolved around work. Was there more to life than that?

With a sigh, she switched on a lamp, grabbed some jeans and a short-sleeve shirt and then made her way to the bathroom to begin her day. She needed to get her thoughts organized as she did when she was working as a detective for the Dallas Police. This wasn't the time to reevaluate her goals.

Five minutes later, she tiptoed past the entrance to the living room where Michael was camped out on the large couch and kept going until she reached the kitchen. Flipping on the overhead light, she scouted the area for some paper and a pen. Usually Aunt Ellen had some on the desktop for phone messages. Kyra rummaged through its drawers and came up empty-handed.

She remembered another place her aunt kept paper, even recalled seeing some tonight when she'd brought Michael some sheets and a pillow to use. The room where Michael was sleeping. But the phone in there was on the desk just inside the entrance. She could take a few paces inside and get the pad. Be out of there in seconds.

She sneaked toward the living room, her breath

bottled in her lungs as she stepped over the threshold. Refusing to even glance toward the couch, she clutched the edge of the desk and felt over its surface until she encountered the pad she needed.

The light from the lamp on the table by the couch flooded the room, and she jumped back.

"Looking for something?" Michael sat on the couch, fully dressed.

"Just came in for some paper. Sorry if I woke you." She backed away a foot, grasping the pad to her chest.

"You didn't. I haven't been asleep for the past hour. I've been sitting here thinking."

"About the case?"

"Among other things." He rose and cut the distance between them. "Why are you up?"

"The case. I can't seem to shut my mind down long enough to sleep any more." She couldn't tell him he was also in her thoughts so much she'd finally gotten out of bed.

"We're certainly a pair."

The idea of them being a pair—a couple—made her shiver. "I can put the coffee on. We can brainstorm together on the case."

Michael trailed behind her toward the kitchen. "I'm not sure I'll be much help. About the only detective work I've done is trying to find the right diagnosis for a patient."

At the counter next to the stove, she put the

coffee packet in the top of the coffeemaker and filled the carafe with water. "It's the same process. You look for clues, go on instinct and experience. You rule out what doesn't fit and finally you come up with the answer—I hope."

"So what are we doing now?"

"Listing what we have and what we need to find out."

"Frankly, I don't know what's going on."

Kyra turned on the pot, then shifted toward Michael. "True. It'll all be conjecture, but that is sometimes what it is at the beginning before we know much."

Michael sat next to her at the table while the scent of brewing coffee saturated the room. "What I know is that Amy is in trouble and running scared."

"Her best friend is supposedly in Tampa, three and a half hours away."

"Someone attacked you tonight. What if it wasn't related to the case?"

"Flamingo Cay hasn't had a mugging in years according to Gabe so I doubt the attack was random."

"Nor has the town had a murder either and now we have two young men dead."

"Shot, but my assailant used a knife." Kyra scribbled down all the things they knew. "I'm not convinced it was the same person. Their height and physique were a little different. I think. Last night happened so fast I can't be totally sure."

"So maybe two people are involved. Great." The corner of his mouth dipped down in a frown.

The action captivated her attention at a time she needed to be professional. She dragged her gaze from his lips to the cleft in his chin, to the unyielding line of his jaw.

"Kyra?"

She looked down at the paper while struggling for a businesslike detachment from the man so close she could caress. "Sorry. Just thinking." She paused, a thought popping into her mind. "The attacker's ski mask smelled of smoke."

"Okay. He smokes."

"Maybe. It could be someone around him who smokes."

"That could mean about a third of the population of Flamingo Cay. Sadly we have a lot of smokers here."

"Still, it could be a clue." Kyra wrote down what she remembered.

"Amy was in the swamp the day before. Is there a connection between the murders and the swamp?"

"I'll put that down on the side of things we need to find out. Along with the motive for killing those two young men. Drugs possibly? We need to see if that dagger tattoo on their necks stood for anything."

"Someone stole Amy's laptop. Why? What was on it that he wanted? What did Amy mean by 'he has my cell phone'? Who? The killer? Someone else?"

"The phone was found on Alligator Island. Any significance to the place?" Kyra went to the stove and poured two mugs of black coffee, then brought them back to the table.

"What's important around here that someone would kill over?"

"The Everglades has had its share of fugitives trying to hide out from the law. I'll ask Gabe about that this morning."

"You know, everything points to the swamp."

"Yeah. Not something I really wanted to hear." She rubbed her palm down her face.

He captured that hand. "Be careful. Your cuts will start bleeding again."

Like a strobe light, images flashed in and out of her mind. Glimpses of what she saw on the finger as the fist came toward her. Gold? Black? Or was that the clothing she was seeing behind the hand? She gave her head a shake.

"What's wrong?"

"Just trying to remember the ring he had on. I'm sure that was what cut my face."

"Although the moon was bright last night, it was still dark outside. Can you be sure of anything?"

"I suppose you're right. It all happened so fast, and the knife was what I really was focusing on."

Michael shuddered. "When I saw you two grappling over it, all I could think of was how big it was."

"Certainly not a kitchen paring knife."

A scowl slashed across his face. His tight voice, clenched jaw conveyed his anger. "You could have been killed."

"I refuse to let the killer stop me. If I did, he's won. Believe me, when it's light, I'll be out there with Gabe looking for any clues to the identity of my attacker."

Straightening, he heaved a deep breath. "Not alone. I'll be out there, too."

"You don't have to. I'll wait for Gabe."

"We're in this together. Remember, I'm to watch out for you and you for me."

The fervent way he said the last sentence brought home how entwined they'd become in this case together in just twenty-four hours. "Then let me help you. Something's bothering you." Her last police partner used to kid her about trying to psychoanalyze him when he had a problem. But when she sensed a person she cared about was hurting, she wanted to help.

"Yeah. Amy's missing."

"No, there's more to it than that. In your own words, you've been driven by your job since you came here. What's driving you? What's going on?"

He looked away, surged to his feet and stalked to the coffeepot and topped off his drink. "You know when you talked about deciding to retire from the police force early because you were tired of seeing so much death and violence? Well, I know what you mean. I've been struggling to decide if I should continue to be a doctor. My decisions and actions can mean the difference between life and death."

"What happened in Chicago?"

"The woman I was going to ask to marry me died because of me."

SEVEN

"What do you mean? What happened to her?" Kyra stood, drawn toward Michael.

He swung around, cradling the mug in between his large palms. Taking a sip, he locked gazes with her. "Sarah and I were going to dinner to celebrate our first-year anniversary dating. I was driving when someone ran a red light and struck us on her side of the car. She lived a little while after the wreck but died at the scene. I couldn't save her."

"So you blame yourself for the fact a man ran a red light and hit you?"

He flinched. His knuckles whitened under the tight clasp on the mug. "It should have been me, not her. I was the one driving. I had the evening all planned. I had reservations at the restaurant at the country inn. I was going to ask her to marry me that night and didn't want to be late. I looked before going out and didn't see he wasn't slowing down. I should have paid more attention. If

I hadn't pulled out into the intersection when the light turned green, she would still be alive."

"When did this happen?"

"A little over a year ago."

"I'm sorry for what happened, Michael. You weren't driving the other car. Sometimes we can't control what occurs. Feeling guilty over surviving won't bring her back, and if she loved you, she wouldn't want you to feel that way."

Michael raised the mug to his lips and sipped, his eyelids veiling his expression.

She touched his upper arm, wanting to do more than that, but his posture warned her to be careful. "Were you hurt?"

"Yes, but nothing life-threatening."

"So you were injured. How did you expect to save her without any medical supplies and yourself hurt?"

"I couldn't even get to her until right before the police showed up. By that time it was all but over with."

"It's a tragedy. No doubt about it. But you weren't responsible for her death. The driver who ran the red light was. After years of training to be a doctor, I hate to see you give up now. I can remember you talking about that when you were growing up. I remember you talking Ginny and me into being your victims so you could practice your first aid."

"Yeah, the first time I bandaged you, you accused me of making you a mummy." His grin lasted a second before falling.

"Your career is just beginning."

He shrugged off her touch and put several feet between them. "Since the wreck, I've been having a hard time dealing with patients dying. In the E.R. I see more of that than some doctors, and it was taking its toll on me."

"When you deal with life-and-death situations sometimes on a daily basis, there will be times when you'll lose someone. I saw that on my job as a cop."

"You finally walked away."

"After twelve years and I'm still a reserve officer, called in if needed in an emergency situation."

"I thought you walked totally away."

"No, not completely. There will always be a part of me that will be a police officer. Like you, I wanted to be one since I was a teen."

"You didn't go far when picking a new job. What a pair we make!"

There was that word again. Pair. So like a couple. The thought didn't send panic through her, which stunned her. "Yeah, like Sherlock Holmes and Dr. Watson."

He chuckled. "I wasn't exactly thinking that kind of pair." Inching closer, he lifted his hand to her face, his eyes a soft blue like the sky on a lazy day. "I'm so glad you chose this week to take a vacation. I'm not sure what I would have done without you here to help. Probably driven Gabe crazy until he decided to lock me in jail for my own safekeeping."

"Now we get to protect each other." Her words came out on a breathless rush while her attention riveted to the feel of his fingers caressing her cheek, jaw, neck.

"Which means we'll have to be together a lot." He bent his head slowly toward hers, his coffee-laced breath fanning over her lips.

She wanted to melt against him. She wanted him to kiss her. She wanted him.

Somewhere in her dazed mind a sound penetrated. The shuffling of shoes on the hardwood floor coming closer to the kitchen. Kyra backed away from Michael as Aunt Ellen entered the room, dressed for the day in matching pants and top, her brown hair neatly fixed, makeup on her face.

"Where are you going today?" Kyra heard the waver in her voice and so did Aunt Ellen by the smug look she gave Kyra.

"Nowhere. With all that's been going on around here, I need to be ready for visitors. Didn't you say something about Gabe coming this morning to check out the beach?"

"Yeah." Was her aunt interested in Gabe? Aunt Ellen had never married although she'd been engaged once, but her fiancé had been killed in the Vietnam War.

A smile curved her mouth as her aunt ambled toward the counter to pour herself some coffee. "There's not a better smell to wake up to. I think I'll go sit on the deck. If I see Gabe, I'll let you know." She waved her hand back at them and added, "Resume what y'all were doing. I didn't mean to interrupt your—work."

Kyra ducked her head, trying to contain her amusement until after her aunt had left the room. The second Aunt Ellen disappeared from view, she released her laugh at the same time Michael did.

"I should have figured something was going on when she got a twinkle in her eye yesterday while talking about besting Gabe at the shooting contest. But I'm not sure the best way to win a man's heart is to beat him at shooting."

"It wouldn't bother me. I probably couldn't hit the wide side of the house standing ten feet away."

"Let's hope you never have to find out."

Michael's eyes grew round. "Me and a gun don't mix. But don't you worry, I'll protect you."

Although he said it with humor beneath the words there was a steel thread, too. He meant it, and she believed him. The declaration gave her a warm, fuzzy feeling in the pit of her stomach. Not something she was used to.

"Do you want something for breakfast?" she asked, wondering how to go about resuming where they were before—inches from kissing. She'd certainly had her share of relationships, but not many in the past few years. She was definitely rusty.

He went and refilled his mug. "Let's wait. Gabe should be here soon. We can get some on the way out of town."

"You aren't a morning person."

"No. I'm used to working the night shift at the hospital in Chicago. It's taken an adjustment to change over to days. I need tons of coffee just to get myself up."

The sound of voices coming from the deck drifted to Kyra. "I think Gabe has arrived." She glanced toward the window over the sink with light streaming through the slits. "Right on time."

"That's Gabe. Should we give Ellen and Gabe a few minutes?"

"Why, Michael Hunt, I do believe you have a romantic streak." She started for the deck.

Michael grabbed her arm and halted her progress, bringing her closer to him. "Actually I do. Once Amy is safe at home and we have time, I want to explore what just happened between us."

"Oh?"

"I'm attracted to you, and I think you return

those feelings. I'm not a young teenage boy anymore with a crush on you."

"You had a crush on me?" she asked in a teasing tone because it had been obvious years ago.

A serious expression darkened his eyes to a navy blue. "Yes, and I know you knew."

His declaration heated her insides—no longer warm and fuzzy. "We'd better go rescue Gabe. My aunt can be a force to be reckoned with."

Michael released her arm, but the brand of his fingers on her skin stayed with her as she made her way toward the back deck. The feel of his gaze on her as she walked flamed her cheeks. He'd been Ginny's kid brother—cute, but with five years between them, she never considered him beyond that. Now five years didn't seem such a gulf as it did back when they were teenagers.

Michael parked in the lot next to Kava Net. The drive to Naples had been filled with a finely honed tension between him and Kyra. He should never have admitted how he'd felt when he was growing up. But a person didn't need to have a genius IQ to have figured it out. Still, he shouldn't have openly admitted it. He'd just been a kid back then. What in the world had possessed him to do that? Kyra. He didn't think straight around her. Hadn't back then and certainly not now.

"I hope something pans out here since Gabe told

us this morning there's no Kip Thomas at the address the person gave when setting up the email account." Michael opened the glass door for Kyra.

"Yeah, and with skullandcrossbones tapping into his account at various commercial places, we may have a hard time tracking the person down. Since this was the last place an email to Amy was sent from, maybe someone will remember the person or they have a tape that can show us him."

"Or her."

"Right. We can't assume anything."

Inside the small café, most of the tables were taken. "Busy little place."

Kyra headed for the counter, offering a huge smile to the young man with a manager's badge on his shirt at the cash register. After showing him her credential from Texas, she leaned toward him and lowered her voice to say, "I could sure use your help. I'm working a case in Flamingo Cay concerning a missing child. One of our leads is an email sent from this location two and a half days ago— late afternoon. Were you working then?"

The man, in his early twenties, straightened and sidestepped to the end of the counter. "Let's talk over here. Yes, I was. What can I do to help you?"

"The email was sent at 4:20 p.m. on Friday. We have some pictures of some people. I want you to take a look and see if you recognize any of them."

Kyra slid the yearbook toward the manager and flipped to the first snapshot of Laurie.

"Yeah, she comes in sometimes."

"How about last Friday?"

"Maybe."

"Okay. How about this one?" She pointed to Preston's picture.

"Yes, ma'am. He's been in here, too."

Kyra showed the manager six more pictures of Amy's friends. He recognized one other, Brady. When she presented Amy's photo to the young man, he couldn't remember ever seeing her. "But you aren't sure about that time on Friday if any of the three you remember were in here?"

"Nope. It was a hectic day. One of my workers didn't show up so I was doing two jobs."

She gestured back toward the door. "Does that camera work?"

"Yes. But the tape is taped over every two days."

"So you don't have any footage of Friday."

He shook his head. "I can't tell you when she came in on Friday with that one," the manager put his finger on Preston's face, "but she did come that day. She has every Friday afternoon since the beginning of summer."

"With him?"

"Sometimes. Sometimes with another guy. Last week it was him."

"How about the other guy?" Kyra turned the page to Brady's picture.

His eyes became slits as he studied Brady for a moment. "I don't think so. He might have been here Friday, but not with her."

"Thanks for your help." Kyra shifted around toward Michael as the manager went back to helping customers. "We need to talk to Laurie, and if she is in Tampa like her mother says, we need to get the contact information and call Laurie. If she isn't skullandcrossbones, that probably leaves either Preston or Brady, and since it doesn't make sense that Amy would email Preston, who she knows is dead, and ask him to meet her, then it's got to be Brady."

"That doesn't make sense, either. Why would she talk about Preston to Brady?"

"It's probably Laurie. But we should talk to Brady, too. His name keeps coming up."

"Let's go. We've got a couple of kids to talk to before the search for Amy begins." Outside the café, he stopped at the car and spoke over the roof. "How is this going to help find Amy?"

"I'm not sure. It might not, but we have to check it out. She took the time to email skullandcrossbones before leaving and set up a meeting. Why? Where?"

Michael opened his driver-side door and climbed into his Saturn. For a few seconds his fingers remained wrapped around the steering wheel as the past twenty-four hours paraded across his mind.

"Are you okay?"

He slanted a look toward Kyra, her face a welcome sight to his tired eyes. "Last night I tried praying to God. I don't know if it did any good."

"It always does good."

"I wish I had your faith."

"You can if you want it."

He unlocked his fingers that were cramping and started the car. "I feel like this past day has been a week."

She touched his arm, drawing his full attention. "Don't give up on praying. If nothing else, tell the Lord your concerns. You don't have to do this alone."

Alone. He'd been alone most of his life. For a brief time Sarah had filled that void, but she'd been taken from him. Now he was back to being alone.

"Cherie's car is here in the driveway," Michael said between ringing the doorbell.

"Maybe she isn't here." Kyra glanced toward the window Laurie's mother had peeked out of the day before. Closed. No sign the woman was home. "Let's check the garage for Laurie's car. We forgot to yesterday."

"She's probably in there like yesterday." Frustration creasing his forehead, Michael opened the screen and pounded on the front door. The third time he struck the wood, the door creaked open. He halted and peered at Kyra. "She always keeps her house locked. Amy told me she was paranoid about it since it was only her and Laurie."

Kyra stepped next to Michael perched on the threshold and leaned toward the opening to listen for any sounds in the house. Inching the crack wider, she yelled, "Mrs. Carson. Laurie." Moving half a foot through the entrance, she cocked her head to the side. "Someone's crying. A baby?"

"Cherie and a baby don't mix. Oh, it's probably their cat, Ringo. Sometimes when Amy has called me, I've heard him carrying on in the background."

Kyra pushed the door completely open. "Listen. He sounds distressed."

The noise came closer until a large white cat ambled down the hallway, whining like a baby the whole way. When he strolled within a few feet of them and stopped, he turned back as if he was going to retrace his steps. That was when Kyra saw blood matted into his fur on his side.

"Michael."

"I see it." Michael charged past Kyra straight for the cat and stooped next to him. "Ringo," he said in a soothing voice.

"Did he hurt himself? Where's Cherie?"

While Michael patted the large male cat, he inspected Ringo for the source of the blood. "I don't feel anything."

Kyra withdrew her gun from her holster. "You stay here. Call Gabe and let him know something's wrong here. I'm checking the house."

She crept down the hall, inspecting each bedroom as she went. No sign of where the blood would have come from. Until she reached the last room.

Kyra rushed into the master bedroom to Cherie lying on the floor, faceup, her swollen eyes closed. Dried blood all over her from small cuts, as though she'd been tortured, intermingled with bruises. Kyra put her finger against the woman's neck. The faint pulse sent relief through Kyra.

"Michael, get in here. Cherie is hurt. Bad."

The pounding of his footsteps announced his hurried approach. He knelt next to Cherie, saying, "Call 911. Get my bag in the car."

Kyra backed away, swung around, then hastened toward the car while phoning 911, then Gabe.

Gabe answered his cell as Kyra grabbed Michael's medical bag. "We're at Cherie Carson's house. We found her near death in her bedroom. It looks like she was beaten and tortured, then left to die."

"I'm on my way. Is Michael with Cherie?"

"Yes. The ambulance from Clear Spring is on its way." Kyra made her way down the hall.

"Don't let anyone else in the crime scene. I'll be there before the ambulance." Gabe clicked off.

Kyra pocketed her phone and gave Michael his bag. "Is she going to make it?"

"I don't know. She's lost a lot of blood. Thankfully most of the cuts have clotted or she would have died hours ago. She's been here awhile."

"I'm going to check the rest of the house. I'm sure the guy is long gone, but I can't assume anything. Gabe will be here soon."

Michael nodded as he began to work on Cherie.

Kyra made her way through the other rooms, opening closets, peering behind a couch—inspecting any place that could conceal a person. Nothing, as she expected, but she did find how the assailant got into the house. He'd cut the glass, raised the window and come through that way. Probably when Cherie was home since the alarm didn't go off. Had the man been there when Michael and she talked with the woman the day before?

Kyra stood on the porch an hour and a half later with Gabe and Michael. "What did Cherie know that she was tortured for?"

"Why was she left alive?" Michael stared through the open front door at the officers still processing the scene.

"A message maybe. If y'all hadn't found her when you did, would she have made it much longer?" Pushing his ball cap back on his head, Gabe chewed on a toothpick.

Michael swung his attention to the police chief. "No. Maybe an hour or so longer. I'm not sure she will make it even now. The doctor at the hospital in Clear Springs will call me with any updates on her status."

"I've asked the sheriff to supply a deputy to keep Cherie under guard."

"She's in a coma. If and when she comes out of it, she may not remember anything that happened. A lot of trauma to the head." Michael's clenched jaw attested to his anger.

Kyra stepped to his side and placed a comforting hand on his shoulder, kneading the tautness beneath her fingers. "Did Cherie know where Laurie was? Is Amy with her daughter?"

"Laurie's car is gone. We know for a fact she isn't at her aunt's in Tampa, and she hasn't been seen in town in the past day. So where is she?" Gabe broke his toothpick in two and stuffed the pieces in his pocket.

"With Amy hiding. They do everything together." Michael propped himself against the porch post, his arms folded over his chest.

"I've put out a BOLO on Laurie's car. We need to go back to their friends and see if anyone knows where they might go." Gabe faced Kyra. "Can you and Michael do that while we search the swamps around here?"

She nodded, glimpsing Michael's scowl deepening. "Did you find the location of those pictures on Amy's camera?"

"No, but I have a few more people to show them to. They will be involved in the search. Right before you called, the sheriff was on his way to meet me at the public pier to help look for Amy and now Laurie. I had Wilson stay and help get everything organized. Wilson called a few minutes ago. They're set to go. I'll leave Connors here to finish up." Gabe started down the steps toward his patrol car. "Call me if you find out anything from their friends." He stopped at his driver-side door. "Watch your backs. Whoever is behind this is deadly serious. If Cherie doesn't pull through, that's a third murder in two days."

The grime expression on Gabe's face hammered home the danger she and Michael were in. This guy, whoever he was, was desperate to find the girls. She prayed he hadn't yet or there would be two more deaths to add to the total.

"I should be out there searching for Amy." The tight thread woven through Michael's voice conveyed his frustration.

"I personally think we'll make more progress talking with the friends. I know you talked with them on the phone yesterday, but I think we should interview them one by one, starting with Brady Lawson. He might be able to tell us where Laurie and Amy would have met up. It sounds like next to Laurie he might know what's going on with Amy since they recently dated."

Michael straightened. "I would have agreed a couple of months ago, but now I don't know if anyone knows who Amy is. Not even Laurie. After we do that, let's go to the hospital. If Cherie comes out of her coma, she may know what we need to find this guy. For all intent and purposes, she shouldn't have been alive. I always felt Cherie had a strong will. Now I know it."

"Let's try Brady's home first. It's only ten-thirty so he may still be asleep."

"Possibly. He works at the movie theater in Clear Springs—usually nights. In the summer they run a late-night movie."

"We need to make her friends see how much danger Amy and Laurie are in." Kyra strode toward Michael's Saturn.

Ten minutes later Michael parked at the curb of a medium-size house painted pink with white shutters. "This is Brady's place."

"Let's show him copies of the photos on Amy's camera. Maybe he'll recognize where they were taken."

Michael marched up to the porch like a man on a mission and rang the doorbell. Drumming his fingers against the wood siding, he waited twenty seconds and pushed the bell again.

The door swung open to reveal a sleepy teenage boy, his hair sticking up. Yawning, he covered his mouth, blinking at the bright light flooding him while behind him his home was dark from heavy curtains drawn. "Dr. Hunt? Have you found Amy?"

"No, that's why we're here." Michael stepped past the teen into the dim foyer.

Kyra followed, and Brady closed the door then faced them.

"I don't know where she is. We broke up a while back. She's…" Brady swallowed the rest of his words.

Michael pinned Brady with an intent look. "She's what?"

The boy drew himself up tall, not taking his gaze from Michael's. "She's different since she started hangin' with Preston."

"How?"

"For starters, she used to hate the color black. Now she wears it all the time."

"I'd like you to look at these photos and see if you know where they were taken." Kyra passed the stack to Brady. "These were on Amy's camera. Some taken a few days ago in the swamp."

Brady reached around her and flipped on the overhead light, then studied each photograph. The wrinkles on his forehead sliced deeper. After finishing, he went back to the second one and held it up. "I think that's Manatee Creek. It gets that way when it rains."

Kyra peered at the picture catching the front end of a kayak making its way through low-hanging branches that almost touched the water's surface. "You can get through there?"

"Yeah, it's not easy but you can maneuver under the mangrove limbs." Brady gave her the photos back. "That's the only one I recognize. I haven't spent much time out in the Glades this summer since I got my job in Clear Springs."

"When's the last time you saw Amy?" Michael's question drew the teen's attention.

"About a week ago. I saw her with Laurie."

"Do you know where Laurie is?"

"Nope. Haven't seen her much, either. Laurie and Amy were doing a lot with Preston and his cousin from Miami. She doesn't have time for us anymore."

Michael tilted his head to the side. "Us?"

"Her old friends."

"Who else should we talk to?"

Brady shrugged. "I guess Hailey. I've seen her with Amy and Laurie lately."

Kyra handed the teen her card. "If you think of anything that might help, call the cell number on here. Amy is in danger. A killer is after her."

Brady's eyes widened. "The same one who murdered Preston and his cousin?"

"Yes."

When they left Brady's place, the drive to Hailey's took only five minutes. Not a word was said in the car, Michael's gaze glued to the road ahead. His jaw clamped in a hard profile. He pulled into the driveway of his partner's house.

"Hailey is Ken's daughter?" Kyra asked as they exited the car.

"Yeah. I'm not sure how much help she'll be since she was on vacation with her family two days ago when Amy spent all day in the swamp. I didn't even call her yesterday morning about Amy going missing since they didn't get back to town until late the night before."

"But maybe she heard from Amy yesterday morning when she ran. Maybe she knows where Amy would have met up with Laurie."

"Right now we could use a big break."

Hailey's mother answered the door, surprised to see Michael. "Ken and I have been so worried about Amy. We've been praying she's found soon." She stepped to the side to allow Kyra and Michael into the house.

"Thanks, Jessica. I'm here to talk to Hailey. Is she home?"

"Yes." When the woman didn't move to go get

her, Michael added, "I want to talk to her about where Amy might go if she was in danger."

Jessica's face went white. "I'll get her."

When Hailey came down the stairs with her mother trailing her, the teen was biting her thumbnail. "Mom thinks I know where Amy is. I don't. I dropped her off at the high-school stadium and that was the last time I saw her."

"You dropped her off at the stadium! When?" The force behind his words caused the young girl to step back. "Sorry. I didn't realize you had, and we've been trying to piece together what happened yesterday morning after Amy found Preston."

"I saw her on Bay Shore Drive and picked her up. She was upset and looked scared, but she wouldn't tell me anything other than that they had seen something they shouldn't have."

"And she didn't tell you what?" Michael opened and closed his hands at his sides.

"She clammed up. Refused to say another word. Sometimes Amy can be melodramatic, and I thought that was one of those times."

"Why didn't you call me about this?" Michael kept his voice calm, but there was nothing calm about his demeanor.

"I didn't realize someone might be after her. I didn't want to get her in trouble."

Kyra pulled out her card and put it into Hailey's

hand. "Call if you remember anything else, especially a place she might go if she wanted to hide." She studied the teen's facial expression to see if she could be keeping anything else a secret. She didn't think Hailey was.

Michael passed the photos to Hailey and asked her to check them and tell them if she knew where any of those places were. The girl hardly looked at the pictures before thrusting them back at Michael. A thunderous expression fell over his features.

"Did you really look?" Kyra asked before Michael said something he would regret. "This is important."

"I don't have to. I stopped doing things with Amy when she started going into the swamp a lot. Not for me." Hailey shivered.

"Did she ever mention anyplace she liked to go?" The tension in Michael slowly leaked away.

"Somewhere beyond Manatee Creek. The only reason I remembered that is I love those animals. But when she started talking about how to get there in detail, my eyes glazed over. She said it was tricky but cool."

"If you remember any other landmarks besides the creek, give us a call." Kyra's cell rang. She turned toward the door and stepped outside on the porch, noticing it was Gabe phoning. "What's up?"

"I just heard Bill Meyers found Laurie's car on

his property in the orchard off Tern Road. He has a big sign saying Meyers Orchard before you turn onto the road that leads to his house. We're pretty far away on the other side of Flamingo Cay in the Glades. Can you go check it out for me? Connors is still tied up with Laurie's house. He'll come out when he gets through. I need to know if there is anything in the car that would point to where the girls went."

"I'll let you know after I see it. We'll head right now to Meyers Orchard."

Michael left Hailey's as Kyra finished the call with Gabe. "Who was that?"

"Gabe. Bill Meyers found Laurie's car on his property. We're going to check it out. But first I want to stop at the drugstore and get some latex gloves."

"Don't have to. I have some in my bag. Did he say anything about how the search was going?"

"At the end, he told me they haven't found anything, and no one recognizes the pictures Amy took."

Using a cane, Bill Meyers led Michael and Kyra toward the orchard trees in back near Big Tern Bay. "I was out here doing a walk-through, checking to make sure the trees weren't infested with bugs, that sort of thing, when I saw the yellow Volkswagen. I called it in, and Gabe told me it was Laurie Carson's. He told me you'd be by. I haven't seen you in years, Kyra."

"Over twenty years. It's good to see you again." She used to come out to his orchard and pick oranges. The fruit tasted so good right off the tree. "You don't have to walk all the way back out there, especially in this heat. Officer Connors will be along later to process the car."

"I'll point him in the right direction, then. When you're through, stop by the house for some freshly squeezed orange juice. You'll probably need it by then." Bill took out a kerchief and wiped his forehead.

"Now that's hard to pass up." Kyra waved goodbye to the seventy-year-old man, then proceeded down the center of the orchard with Michael, heading toward the bay.

A couple of terns the bay was named after flew overhead, their screeches piercing in the thick, humid afternoon air. Through the grove of orange trees Kyra spied the round yellow back of the Volkswagen.

"Why did they come here?" Michael slanted a look at Kyra.

"There's a pier in the bay down that incline. Bill used to have a few boats tied up there. Probably not now but maybe. We can ask him later."

"So Amy and Laurie could have taken one of his boats." The incredulous tone in his voice underscored how upset he was. "I can't believe everything Ginny worked with Amy on has been forgotten so quickly. She used to be naive, think before she did something. Respect authority."

Kyra stopped twenty yards away from the car and faced Michael. "She's scared. She's doing all she can to stay alive." But she couldn't help but wonder what was keeping Amy from seeking help from the police. Was she involved in something with this case?

"I know." His shoulders sagged. "I'm just frustrated I can't help her. That she's alone in all of this."

"She's not alone."

"Yeah. Yeah. The Lord is with her."

"Well, yes, but so is Laurie or at least I hope so. Otherwise where is Laurie?"

"That's a good question." Michael skirted Kyra and hurried toward the car.

Out the corner of her eye, she glimpsed a movement and whirled toward where she saw it. Nothing was there. She started forward. But with each step she took, she couldn't shake the sensation someone was out there, watching.

When Michael was a few feet from the car, she called out, "Stop."

Instinct compelled her to leap toward Michael

and haul him back. An explosion rocked the earth beneath her, sending Michael and her flying through the air. A bone-jarring landing knocked the breath from her lungs as Michael flung himself on top of her while bits of the car rained down on them.

EIGHT

For a few seconds the press of Michael's body into hers further robbed her of a decent breath. The sound of the explosion deafened her ears. The heat from the blast seared her. A column of smoke and fire shot upward toward the sky while some flaming pieces of the car fell back to earth. One landed a foot from her.

Kyra shoved at Michael. "Someone blew up the VW."

He rolled to the side, a dazed look on his face.

Although the concussion from the explosion muffled her hearing, Kyra scrambled to her feet, drawing her gun. The sudden action made her wobble, but she managed to steady herself before sinking back to the ground. "Let's get out of here." Waving him behind her, she faced the area where she thought she'd seen something, determined to keep them safe. Had someone rigged the car to blow up? Had they been waiting for them or was the bomb set on a timer?

Was he still here? Waiting to pick them off if they survived the blast?

She glimpsed something green that wasn't part of a plant. She kept her gun pointed in the general area of the threat. At least she hoped so. Chancing a sweep of the terrain, she discovered a down tree five feet to the left.

"Over there." She gestured with her hand that didn't hold her Glock toward the log and brush that could give them some cover.

Michael dived for the protection ten seconds before she followed. Half expecting a bullet in the back, Kyra made it safely behind the fallen tree, then pulled out her cell. First she called 911 to get the fire department out to Bill's. Then she dialed Gabe. As she reported what happened to them, Bill came down the center row toward the car.

Michael saw him and, stooping low, ran toward the old man. "Get back. Not safe."

"Got to go." Kyra clicked off and kept her attention trained on the foliage around the VW for any sign of an assailant or gun, hoping to cover Michael as much as possible.

Michael reached Bill, put his arm around him and hurried the older man toward a shelter of trees. Kyra released a long breath when they were hidden from view, down on the ground. Her cell rang, but she didn't dare take her attention off the area where she suspected someone was hiding. Her heart hammered a fast beat against her rib cage and thundered in her ears, almost drowning out the sound of the sirens in the distance.

The blaze engulfed the car totally. Two orange trees near by caught fire. Flames licked their way through the branches. Smoke roiled into the sky, fingering outward toward Kyra. The fiery heat scorched the air. And still she didn't want to stop her vigil. She didn't think the man would still be around, especially since help was on its way, but she couldn't take the chance. She was the one with the gun. She had to protect Michael and Bill.

Her eyes trained on the bushes across from her stung. She coughed, her throat dry, closing up. When flames surrounding the VW began to expand outward, chewing up the grass and foliage, she knew she couldn't stay put any longer. She had to make a run for it and pray the assailant had done the same thing. It was suicide otherwise.

Behind her were rows and rows of orange trees. She could escape that way and skirt back around to make sure Michael and Bill got away safely. Hugging the ground as close as she could, she ran deeper into the grove, away from the bay, away from the burning car.

Michael ducked his head up to see what was happening. Where was Kyra? Was she safe? Over the crackles of the fire, he hadn't heard any gunshots. But if there was someone out there by the car, at least Kyra had a weapon. She was trained and could take care of herself. Why didn't that make him feel any better?

"What's going on?" Bill asked, stooping down on the ground by the base of his tree several feet away from Michael.

His gaze connected with the old man's, full of terror, the wrinkles on Bill's face more pronounced. "The car blew up."

"It looked fine when I checked it out."

"How long ago?"

"An hour and a half ago. I called the police station and talked to the dispatcher. I thought someone would be out here sooner from what she'd said. Then I remembered the search for your sister this morning, so I figured that was why there was a delay. I was kinda surprised to see you here."

Why had it taken so long for Gabe to call Kyra? So many questions plagued him. "The fire is spreading. We've got to move back. The problem is someone set an explosion, and that person could still be around."

"Whatever for and who is he?"

"Both good questions. I don't have answers for either one."

The blare of sirens grew closer. Michael peered over to where Kyra was holed up. The fire inched nearer to her location. Smoke swirled and mushroomed from the blast. From his angle he could see her back away from the log then swing around and crouch down to hurry away.

"Let's get out of here, Bill. Stay there. I'll come to you. We'll need to move fast."

Lord, we could use Your help.

Michael darted to Bill and helped him to his feet. Supporting some of the older man's weight, Michael started toward the edge of the orchard. Bill stumbled and went down, toppling both of them.

Kyra met Connors and the fire trucks as they came into the yard. While the firefighters began setting up to contain the blaze, she turned to Connors. "The car exploded right before we reached it. If I hadn't thought I saw something in the bushes, we could have been closer and not made it out alive."

"Where's Dr. Hunt?"

"I saw them heading this way. They should be here by now." She pivoted to scour the area for them. Did the assailant stay after all and somehow get to Michael and Bill? With the sounds of the fire and sirens, a shot could be masked, especially if he used a silencer. She started toward the smoke-filled orchard.

"Where are you going?" Connors asked.

"After them. They might be in trouble."

Urgency quickened her steps. She heard a firefighter behind her yell at her to stop, but she kept going into the grove. She had told Michael she would protect him. He'd covered her when the car exploded and had taken the brunt of the raining bits of car. He'd risked his life for her. The least he deserved was her returning the favor.

Pulling the collar of her shirt over her mouth and nose, she rushed toward the area where she'd last seen Michael and Bill. Through the haze of smoke she saw two bodies down on the ground. The sight surged her pace, adrenaline pumping through her veins.

A few feet away Michael shoved himself up, locking gazes with her. Relief momentarily gleamed in his eyes before he swept his attention to Bill still down. He scrambled toward the old man, who moved his head around to look at Michael. Bill groaned.

"What happened?" Kyra knelt beside them.

"We were hurrying. Bill tripped and we went down. Where do you hurt?" Michael asked Bill as he checked his body.

"Ankle. I think I twisted it or something."

"We've gotta get both of you out of here. The fire is spreading." A series of coughs racked her body.

The sound of the fire grew nearer, louder. Through the smoke, flames lit the earth, devouring anything in their way.

Michael rose and assisted Bill to his feet. Michael wrapped his arms around the old man and bore most of his weight. Kyra led the way, scanning their path ahead for any signs the blaze had cropped up in front of them or for the person who set the bomb in the VW.

As they emerged from the orchard, Connors hurried up to them and helped Michael with Bill. "The fire chief wants us to get back. Bill, your house should be all right for now. The wind is blowing in the opposite direction, but a firefighter hosed it down just in case."

"Let's get him to my car. I need to get him to the clinic."

"Shouldn't you all be checked for smoke inhalation?" Connors said as Bill coughed.

Kyra's throat burned and her chest felt tight. She couldn't understand why anyone would smoke and breathe in this stuff willingly. That thought again reminded her of her assailant last night. Did he smoke or was he around someone who did?

"I've got everything we need back at the clinic. I can be there in ten minutes."

Kyra rushed forward and opened the back door to Michael's car. "Why don't I drive in case Bill needs you."

"Child, I'll be fine. Just a twisted ankle. I'll be hopping around in a few days," Bill protested.

Michael chuckled. "You might want to wait a

little longer than that. Let's get an X-ray first and some oxygen. Then you can go out dancing if you want."

When the two men were settled in the backseat, Kyra switched on the engine and pulled away from Bill's house. In the rearview mirror her attention fixed on the smoke and flames bellowing into the sky. Someone hadn't wanted them to see the car. Why? Or was it something else? A way to stop Michael and her? If so, how did he know they were coming to look at the VW? Did Bill tell anyone else but the dispatcher and Gabe?

Kyra let Gabe into her place and gestured toward the great room. As she shut the door, lightning streaked across the sky. Dark clouds hung low, menacingly. It was five and it looked like nighttime over two hours early. Thunder rocked the house as she and Gabe made their way into the room where Michael and Aunt Ellen were.

"I pray Amy and Laurie are inside somewhere protected. This isn't going to be a gentle summer shower," Kyra said in a low voice to Gabe at the entrance.

"I was hoping the tropical storm Edna would bypass us totally, but it looks like we're getting the western edge." He frowned, his gaze straying to the picture window that overlooked the beach and gulf.

Whitecaps covered the water for as far as Kyra could see. Palms swayed in the wind. Another flash of lightning lit up the dark immediately followed by a loud clap of thunder.

Kyra sought Michael in the great room. His eyebrows swept downward, his mouth pressed in a tight line. The haunted expression in his eyes ripped at her. By the time he finished at the clinic with Bill as well as himself and her, the tropical storm was moving in and Gabe had called to tell him they were coming back to Flamingo Cay early. Even knowing about the storm, Michael had been determined to go out in his partner's airboat and do some searching. But the coast guard had issued a small-craft warning.

Michael surged to his feet and strode to the window, staring outside, his hands stuffed in his pockets. "This doesn't look good."

Gabe moved farther into the room. "It should blow through quickly. We can be back out tomorrow looking for Amy. Finding Laurie's car means they are most likely around here somewhere. If that's the case, we'll find them. I'll be going over the map tonight with Wilson and Nichols. Certain areas will have priority over others."

Michael pivoted, his back to the window. "Her friends couldn't really help. No one recognized the places in the photos. Hailey said Amy mentioned a place around Manatee Creek."

The view of him in plain sight for anyone out on the beach made Kyra uncomfortable. She cut the distance between them and shut the drapes. "No reason to take any chances." Everything was escalating. The bombing wrenched up the stakes even higher.

Gabe removed his ball cap and took a seat on the couch with Aunt Ellen. "That's almost two hours away by boat. It's a pretty desolate area."

"But maybe a great place to hide." Kyra sat in a lounge chair across from Gabe. "They don't have a car anymore. If Amy is comfortable in the swamp, then I could see her fleeing there to hide."

"We've finished covering the area around Alligator Island. We'll expand our search tomorrow. Take a look at the Glades between Flamingo Cay and Manatee Creek."

"How about Tern Bay? There was a dock down below the orchard. Did Amy and Laurie escape that way after abandoning the car? Bill said he kept a couple of boats at his pier. That needs to be checked on tomorrow." Michael tousled his hair with his fingers. "I still don't understand the car being at the orchard. That's in the opposite direction from Manatee Creek. What if someone else moved it there and laid a trap for us? The car blew up as we approached. We'd have been caught in the blast if Kyra hadn't stopped when she did and pulled me back."

"Oh, dear, do you think someone was waiting for you before detonating the bomb?" Aunt Ellen shifted a few inches closer to Gabe on the couch.

"Right before I got here, the fire chief told me it looks like that was what happened, but nothing is official until an investigator can check the car out thoroughly. Or at least what is left of it."

"How's Bill's orchard?" Aunt Ellen asked.

"He lost about fifty percent of his trees in that orchard. He has two more orchards on the other side of his house."

"I'm going to have to bake him some cookies. That ought to raise his spirits a bit. People always seem glad to get a batch. Did he go home?"

"Ken was taking him home after his last breathing treatment. Thankfully his house wasn't affected by the fire." Michael paced the room. "Before coming back here, Kyra and I went to the hospital in Clear Springs. Cherie stirred some, but she hadn't come out of her coma. Her chances, though, have improved throughout the day. The doctor took her off the critical list this afternoon."

Aunt Ellen put her hands on her thighs and stood. "Well, I hope y'all are starved. I made some spaghetti. Gabe, I hope you'll stay tonight."

The police chief grinned. "A home-cooked meal. You won't see me turn down one when offered. Can I help you?"

"Sure. You can set the table while I put the French bread in the oven and throw together a salad."

"I love spaghetti. Have I ever told you I'm a fourth-generation Italian on my mother's side. She used to make the best spaghetti and…" Gabe's voice faded the further into the kitchen he went.

"Should I warn Gabe?" Kyra asked with a chuckle.

"What about?"

"Aunt Ellen's cooking. I definitely should call Bill about the cookies she wants to bring him."

"It can't be that bad." Michael took a whiff of the air. "It smells good."

"Maybe she's improved. Dad used to complain all the time to me about her cooking, but he couldn't bring himself to say anything to her. She got such pleasure out of it. You would think after years she would have gotten better from doing it so many times."

"Nah. You shouldn't say anything to Gabe. He may love what she fixes." Michael walked to the drapes over the picture window and fingered them apart a few inches. "It's really coming down now. I thought about trying to call Ginny to let her know what's going on with Amy, but I know she was leaving for the interior and wouldn't be available until next weekend when she returns to the mission."

"Hopefully by next week everything will be over and Amy will be back home safe."

He threw a glance at her. "You really feel that way? She has a killer after her who has now decided we are his target, too. She's caught up in something we don't know anything about. She's probably out in the Glades in this thunderstorm. Doesn't look too good to me."

"I've got to believe she'll be all right. Once I begin buying into the fact Amy isn't then that's when things turn for the worse."

"Hey, I was always the optimistic one. You were the pessimistic one. What's changed you?"

"When I came to believe in the Lord wholeheartedly, I realized He's my strength. He gives me hope. Hope is what keeps me going forward. What caused you to change?"

Michael's gaze cut through her. A faraway look entered his eyes. "After the first couple of patients I lost in the E.R., I began to feel helpless. When I couldn't save Sarah, I couldn't understand why all my years of training went for nothing. I'd wanted to spend the rest of my years with her, and there was nothing I could do to keep her alive."

"It was her time to go. You don't have a say in that."

He faced her. "I know it in here—" he tapped his temple "—but I'm having a hard time understanding it in here." He splayed his hand over his heart.

"You're fighting for control. Ultimately the Lord is in control. When you realize that, you'll come out the winner."

Laughter drifted to them from the kitchen. Kyra peered behind her toward the door that led into that room. "I think we'd better go break up those two."

Michael inhaled deeply. "Yeah, I think the bread is burning."

Not able to sleep beyond a few hours, Michael paced the den, plowing his fingers through his hair. He walked to the drapes and looked out the slit. The rain had finally stopped around three in the morning, but the wind still blew enough to whip the palm fronds like flags. Nothing was going to stop him from being involved in the search for Amy today.

He could feel his little sister's fear. He imagined her shivering in the cool, wet night air. She knew the swamp, but he doubted she could avoid a killer for long or for that matter survive for long in the desolate part of the Everglades where he thought she might have gone. Creeks that were hard to travel down. Tangled mangroves choking the other vegetation. Muddy bogs that slowed a person's progress. Predators that usually stayed away from humans until they came into their territory.

And Amy was in the middle of it. Gabe and his

officers had done a thorough search of Flamingo Cay. The whole town was on the lookout for his sister and Laurie. They weren't here. They were out there in the Glades.

Streaks of light ushered the coming of dawn. He'd already talked with Ken about using his airboat to take him as far as he could go with it. Then he was going to use his kayak for the less navigable waterways around Manatee Creek.

While he waited for morning, restlessness agitated him. He shouldn't go outside, but the walls pressed in on him. He opened the French doors and stepped out onto the back deck. The wind created large waves that crashed against the shore. The tails of his short-sleeve shirt caught on the breeze and whipped about him. Humidity hung thick in the air.

He strolled to the railing and leaned into it, taking deep breaths of the cool, salty air. Later it would feel miserably hot when the sun came out, but for now he enjoyed the refreshing start to the day.

When his cell rang, the sound startled him, and he jerked back, quickly digging in his pocket for the phone. He didn't recognize the number as he answered, "Yes?"

"Michael, I'm in trouble and don't know what to do." Amy's frightened voice scared him more than her words.

NINE

"Where are you? I'm coming to get you. I'll keep you safe." Michael prayed that was possible, especially after the near miss today with the car explosion.

"You can't tell anyone where I am, especially the police."

"Why?" The feel of eyes on him slithered down his length. He strode toward the French doors and reentered the house, then turned the lock. "What's going on, Amy?"

"The man after me is being protected by a cop. I heard him say that. I don't know who. Please promise me you won't let the police know where I am."

The plea in his sister's voice ripped at his composure. Michael sank onto the couch where he'd slept earlier. "I won't."

"It's where we went exploring and found that old Native American burial ground near Winn River."

"You went that far from here?"

"It's the only really isolated place I know. I'm

not there yet. We just entered the creek and cell reception is going. Our canoe has several holes in it from hitting logs, but I think we can make it. Laurie and me will be in the hut near the burial ground. I didn't know where else to hide." Tears laced her voice. The last word ended on a sob.

"I'm on my way. We'll talk when I get there. I'm not going to let anything happen to you or Laurie."

"Please hurry. He could find us again."

"Again?" Panic bolted through Michael.

"Yes, we were trying to leave town, and he followed us. We had to abandon Laurie's car and barely escaped getting caught by…"

Her voice faded in and out. "Amy? Are you there?"

"Yes," she cried.

"Do you know the man after you?"

"Never seen—him before three days—"

Their connection went dead. The panic Michael had tried to hold at bay ran rampant through him as he surged to his feet. For a few seconds, he stood frozen, unable to think or do anything.

Then quickly plans began to form in his mind. He would sneak out of Kyra's house and leave Ken's pier before anyone else knew what he was doing. He would take his kayak with him because there were only places a paddleboat could go on the last part of the trip. He didn't want to put Kyra in any more danger. She could have died today in the orchard, not to mention what had happened to her the night before on the beach. A few more feet and the blast would have done some serious damage. As it was she'd been cut from flying debris, and he had stitched up several of her wounds. Her last few encounters had made her look as if she'd been in a street fight and lost. All of this was because of what his kid sister had gotten caught up in. Because he had asked her to help.

He would need to go home to pick up some equipment, but he should be at Ken's right at dawn. When he spied some paper on the desk in the great room, he snatched a piece and scribbled a note to Kyra, pleading with her not to even let Gabe know that he had gone after Amy, that he would explain everything later. Then he headed toward the French doors.

"Michael, where are you going?"

With his back to her, he gripped the handle, trying to think of a way to leave without arousing her suspicion. He didn't want to endanger her life any more than he already had. Yes, she could take care of herself, but he'd lost Sarah and hadn't been able to do a thing to help her. He couldn't take it if it happened again to him. In that moment he realized he cared for Kyra—that what he felt as a teenager had not diminished over the years.

"Michael?"

The worry he heard in her voice gutted him. "I

need to go to my house for something. I'll be back in a while." He didn't turn around, not wanting her to see anything in his expression.

"I'll walk with you. I love the beach at this time of day."

Slowly he rotated toward her. "I'm going alone."

"It might not be safe." She touched the gun in her holster at her waist. "Remember, we're watching out for each other."

That's why I'm going alone. He wanted to tell her that, but he knew by the tight set of her lips and slight narrowing of her eyes that no matter what she would be coming with him.

"What do you need to get? Maybe we have it here."

He averted his gaze for a long moment, his teeth grinding. "Amy called me a few minutes ago."

"That's great. Where is she?"

"By Winn River. A place we went several years ago."

"So we can go get her. Gabe will be relieved." Kyra pulled out her cell.

Michael covered her hand on the phone with his. "No. You can't call him."

Deep creases grooved her forehead. "Why?"

"Amy made me promise not to. She is sure a police officer is helping the killer."

"Who?"

"She didn't know. Something the killer said that made her feel that way."

"So she doesn't really know?"

"No, but what if it's true?"

"Gabe can keep it a secret."

Michael drilled his gaze into her. "What if it is Gabe?"

Kyra's mouth dropped open. "No, not Gabe. I know him. He'd never do something like that."

"I'm not taking any chances with my sister's life. My first and only priority at this time is to bring Amy home safely."

"I told you from the beginning I would protect Amy. If that's what you want to do, then I won't say anything to Gabe. My priority is to keep her safe—whatever it takes. But for the record, it isn't Gabe."

"I don't think it's Gabe either, but I can't take the chance I'm wrong." He'd done enough of that lately—making mistakes. He couldn't afford to make more—not with Amy's life. Not with Kyra's life. "I want to get some equipment at my house. We'll take Ken's airboat then use my two-man kayak to go the last part of the trip. We'll tow Amy's kayak. It's a long trip."

"Then let's get going."

As Michael emerged from the house, Kyra went into bodyguard mode. As she scanned the terrain, he did, too. Every dark shadow became a menacing form. Where was the killer? He would have to keep an eye out behind him as well as in front of him in the swamp. He could easily imagine the man nearby watching their every move.

As they entered the creek from the river, Kyra couldn't inhale enough air to ease the pressure in her chest. The canopy of trees above them created dark shadows over the terrain and water before them. The dense mangrove banks on either side sent branchy fingers out toward them as though to trap them in their wooden talons. The constant buzz of insects crowded out all other sounds until a scurrying noise to the left punctured the clamor. Kyra shifted her focus toward the racket. A raccoon hurried into the thicket.

Sweat poured off her. Mosquitoes attacked her even though she'd slathered insect repellant all over her. At least the ceiling of flora above her gave some relief from the heat and strong sunlight that had beat down on them on the river. Dipping her paddle into the coffee-colored water, she followed the narrow path that Michael made in the boat ahead of her.

She removed her hat and stuffed it down into the kayak when she saw Michael duck under a low-hung ceiling of limbs. "Are you sure this is the way? It looks impassable."

"That's the beauty of the place. Not a lot of people come this way."

"Do you see those broken branches? Someone has come this way recently."

"Yes, Amy and Laurie."

Amy and Laurie or someone else following the girls?

The question played over and over in her mind as she paddled deeper into the tangle for the next half hour. The niggling sensation that had plagued her since they'd started earlier this morning from Ken's pier still nipped at her like the mosquitoes letting her know they weren't going away.

Slowly the thick foliage thinned until Kyra had to don her hat again to protect her face from the strong sun rays. They had been in the Glades over three hours when Michael headed toward a break in the trees.

"We'll walk from here." Michael brought his kayak as close as he could and tied it to a branch, then climbed from the craft and waded a few steps to more solid ground.

In Amy's boat, Kyra followed suit, inspecting her surroundings for any signs of something not right. After sloshing through the foot-deep water to the higher bank, she inhaled the humidity-saturated air and released it slowly through pursed lips.

"It's not far from here." Michael began his hike

through the vegetation, pausing to check out a canoe stashed between some bushes, barely visible.

When he pushed back some limbs, Kyra spied holes in the boat. "I can't believe they made it this far."

"She said they ran over some logs. I can't believe she got a call through to me."

"The Lord is looking out for them."

Michael threw her a look, his head tilted. He started to say something, closed his mouth shut and continued down the narrow path toward the Native American burial ground. Mud and patches of water hindered their progress, but finally fifteen minutes later a small clearing opened up before Kyra.

An eerie silence blanketed the site. Off to the side sat a dilapidated shack that would completely fall down in the next high wind. Amy flew out through the opening where the door once was and launched herself toward Michael, who scooped her up into his arms.

Tears streaked down the teenage girl's cheeks. "You came. I didn't expect you for a while, but…" Amy pulled back and peered at Kyra. The girl's forehead crinkled, and her eyes narrowed as she tried to place who Kyra was. "I thought you were coming alone."

She smiled at Amy. "I haven't seen you in years, but you've grown up into a beautiful young lady.

I'm Kyra, Ginny and Michael's friend. He asked for my help."

"You were at the house," Amy mumbled, then glanced up at Michael. "You promised you wouldn't tell anyone."

"You didn't want me to tell the police. I didn't, but Kyra has been helping me look for you. She used to be a detective with the Dallas Police. Now she runs a bodyguard agency. She's here to protect you. I trust her."

Those three words cloaked Kyra in a mantle of warmth that had nothing to do with the temperature.

"Ginny used to talk about you all the time." Acceptance inched into Amy's expression. "We can certainly use all the help we can get."

"You've got it. We're going to figure out what's going on." Had the Lord put her in the place where she could help Michael and Amy? What would have happened to the child if Kyra hadn't been on that beach that morning when the two guys were killed? She shivered at the thought of another victim being added to the killer's total.

Behind sister and brother stood Laurie in the opening to the hut. Dark shadows under the child's eyes reminded Kyra of the raccoon she'd seen. Terror marked every feature of Laurie's face. She clasped the edge of the hut as though that was the only thing keeping her upright.

Kyra covered the short distance to her. "I'm here to help you, too. I will protect you as well as Amy."

Laurie's eyes fastened on the gun at Kyra's waist and widened. Amy's friend opened her mouth, but no words came out. Kyra took the frightened teen into her embrace and hugged her trembling body against her. Laurie sobbed. Kyra tightened her arms around her to keep the girl from collapsing to the ground.

Michael stepped back a pace and looked at Amy. "What's going on? Why is a madman after you two? What's this about the guy after you being protected by a cop?"

"I'm not sure what is really going on. The four of us—myself, Laurie, Preston and Tyler—were exploring up by Manatee Creek. We got turned around and lost for a while. We came upon a small island with an abandoned cabin on it." Amy paused and gulped in a deep breath. "But it wasn't deserted. Someone was living in it."

"And he came after you because you showed up?" Michael's eyebrows slashed downward.

"Not exactly. He wasn't there at first. We went inside and looked around. When we heard him coming, we ran."

"So he saw you and ran after you all?"

Laurie stiffened against Kyra. "He was with another man—tall and thin, creepy-looking. They were arguing and the guy whose stuff was in the cabin said that a cop was protecting him and everything would be all right. He'd done jobs like this all the time."

"Jobs like what?" Kyra glanced from Amy to Laurie.

Amy shook her head. "He didn't say, but the tall, thin man wasn't convinced everything would be all right. They exchanged a few more words and the thin man left while the other guy came toward the cabin. We ran. In my rush, I must have dropped my phone. I was taking pictures with it. That must have been how he tracked us down. All my information and friends are in it."

"You two ready? I want to leave right away. It's a long trip home," Michael said, plastering his sister against his length, protecting her in the shelter of his arm. "We'll figure this all out when we get back to Flamingo Cay."

"The last part of the trip our canoe took on so much water, we had to wade the rest of the way here. We dragged it with us. I didn't want anyone to see it submerged in case he was…" Shaking her head, Amy swallowed hard, tears glistening in her eyes. "He found us twice—at the Pattersons' and when we tried to leave town. I can't…" She buried her face into Michael's shoulder.

He stroked Amy's back. "You aren't alone anymore."

His gaze captured Kyra's and across the small

clearing a connection leaped between them that Kyra had never felt before. Its impact stunned her. Not until Laurie stepped back into the hut to grab their belongings did Kyra realize how easily Michael's presence could distract her. At the worst possible time when lives hung in the balance.

"Let's go," Kyra said, forcing herself to avert her attention from him. "I don't want to be out here after dark."

As they neared the mouth of the creek, Michael glanced back at Kyra and Laurie in the kayak behind him. Laurie looked shell-shocked, while Kyra kept the boat going forward with deep strokes of the paddle. He couldn't have asked for a better partner than her.

"Michael," Kyra called out, "let me go first now. I know we're near the river. I want to check the area out first before we approach the airboat."

"Fine." He slowed his craft and moved as closed to the bank as he could with the submerged trees and logs. "It's around the next bend. You'll have a little room before you go out into the river."

She steered past him. "Stay back. I know we hid the airboat on the other bank in a stream, but we still need to be cautious."

She was right. The killer after Amy and Laurie would stop at nothing to find them. He still didn't know why. If they could figure that out, maybe they could discover who was after the girls. Once they made it to the airboat, they could be back in Flamingo Cay in two hours, then they could start trying to piece together what was going on.

Shielding herself behind a wall of foliage, Kyra used the binoculars she'd had him bring to scout out the area across the river where another creek emptied into it.

"Do you think someone followed you?" Amy asked behind him.

"We kept an eye out as we made our way here, but Kyra has been trained to check out every contingency." Michael glimpsed the tensing of Kyra's shoulders as she took another look through the binoculars.

Then she turned the kayak in a tight circle and paddled back to him. "Something doesn't feel right. I thought I saw the tip of a boat hidden a little farther down the stream. I would have missed it totally if it wasn't for something that glinted in the sunlight. I hate to ask this, but is there another way out of here besides going out onto this river right here?"

"You mean we're trapped!" Laurie spoke—a high-pitched shrill of hysteria in her voice—for the first time since they started down the creek.

Amy reached across the short distance that separated the two kayaks and took her friend's hand. "No, Michael will find another way out of here."

Then his sister turned her appealing gaze on him. He visualized the charts of this portion of the Glades that he'd reviewed right before heading out, then he thought back to a few months ago when Amy and he had come to this place—a lifetime ago when they were settling into a brother-sister relationship.

"We need to go back the way we came. Continue up the creek. It ends but not too far from another stream we can take to another river that empties into the canal close to Flamingo Cay near Egret Bay." At least he hoped so. Charts could become outdated with the changing water flow or a hurricane.

Laurie pointed a shaking hand in the direction they would have to travel. "We have to go back there. What about the stories about Jaws?"

"What stories?" Kyra gave Michael a quizzical look.

"Lately people have been reporting about an overly aggressive alligator there. A bull gator that is reported to be about sixteen feet long."

Amy tugged on her friend's hand, drawing Laurie's attention around to her. "We'll be in these boats. Alligators usually don't attack people. I haven't heard anything lately. We should be fine and by that time not far from home."

"Let's go. We need to get as far as we can before dark. If we can make the other river, we can travel at night and get back to town before it gets too late. The weather report I heard said another storm was moving in late tonight." Michael maneuvered his kayak around and started the trip back up the creek.

Lord, if You're listening, please help us. Show us the way.

Two hours later the creek seemed to come to an end with a barrier of green in every direction he turned.

"We're trapped!" Laurie cried out, her hands gripping the edge of the kayak.

TEN

Kyra twisted around to settle Laurie down, reaching back to grasp her hands. "Calm down."

The teen yanked away from her, rocking the kayak. The motion of the boat fueled Laurie's panic, and she tried to stand up. The boat rolled over, sending Kyra and the girl into the muddy creek. The seventeen-year-old's screams died down when Laurie went under, then surfaced splashing and spewing out water.

Michael guided his kayak closer to grab for Laurie and have her cling to its side. Kyra blocked the fact she was in the creek up to her shoulders and grabbed hold of her craft to flip it back over—glad that most of their equipment was in Michael's bigger boat. She struggled to get it righted. Before she realized, Michael was in the water next to her, helping her to turn the boat over. When it was settled in place, Kyra scanned the area for the paddle and found it had drifted under the coiling branches of the mangrove.

While Michael assisted Laurie into the kayak, heaving her up into it, Kyra swam the few yards to snag the paddle and bring it back. Her fingers encircled the wooden handle at the same time a large snake dropped into the creek from the branches above and headed straight for her. All she could focus on was its large head, the size of a fist, and its flicking tongue as its dark beady eyes knifed through her composure.

She quickly drew the paddle toward her to use as a weapon while saying, "Michael! A snake!"

"Move. Back."

As the snake came closer, Kyra backpedaled toward the kayak, keeping the paddle between her and the long reptile. Her heart pounded so hard it was difficult to breathe. Her gaze skimmed down its length, and she estimated it was at least ten or twelve feet long with a thick body. A python? In the Glades? Not poisonous but not something she would want to tangle with. She shoved all the snake stories she'd heard to the background and used the paddle as a shield.

The snake slithered within a few feet of her but no closer as it continued to swim across to the other bank. Kyra didn't take her eyes off it until it slipped out of the creek and she lost sight of it in the dense foliage. Her pulse still speeding through her, she wilted back against the boat, her legs going weak.

Michael grabbed her and held her up, hauling her close to him. "You okay?"

"No, give me a sec," she squeaked out between deep gasps of air while a chill encased her. She quivered in his embrace, and he tightened his hold.

"It's gone. It was probably more scared of you than you were of it."

"I doubt that," she said with a laugh that fell flat. "What's a python doing in the Everglades? It's not native to here."

"There are a lot of them now. Pets people have released into the wild."

"Oh, great. As if there aren't enough snakes in this swamp." The feel of his arms around her calmed her until she managed to stop shivering. The beating of her heart slowed. Glancing around, she stepped away and gripped the boat. "Let's get out of here in case it has a buddy. I think we can get through the creek there." She pointed toward the area where the paddle had been.

Michael examined the mangrove wall. "It'll be tight, but I think we can. Here, I'll help you up."

With his hands around her waist, she jumped and drew herself into the kayak. Although it was hot in the shade of the creek, her soaked clothes left her cold. Teeth chattering, she settled into the craft and took the paddle he gave her. A putrid aroma emanated from her wet clothes.

Michael sidestepped along the kayak until he

was next to Laurie. Tears ran down her cheeks. She swiped her hand across her face.

"Laurie, pull yourself together. We can't have a repeat of that. Do not stand up in the kayak or rock it." Michael's stern voice riveted the girl's attention.

"I'm sorry. I…" Laurie lowered her head and stared at a spot in front of her.

"We'll get home. But we have to work together." With a frown, Michael waded to his boat.

Kyra peered over her shoulder at the teenage girl. "You're going to be okay. I'm not going to let anything happen to you."

Laurie raised her head. "I didn't mean to tip the boat over." Her voice quavered on the last word.

"I know." Kyra sent her a smile she hoped reassured Laurie.

The sun disappeared behind the trees along the western shore of the river. Michael paddled a few feet in front and to the side of Kyra. "How much farther?"

"A little more to Egret Bay then the canal to Flamingo Cay isn't too much beyond that."

"Will we be home before dark?" Laurie's hands gripped the sides of the boat.

Michael looked back at Amy's friend. "No, probably not for another hour or two, but that will be better for us since we don't want anyone to know you all are back in town. We'll need to lie low until we figure out what's going on."

"What about Jaws? Don't alligators like to feed at night?" Laurie's eyes grew round as she panned the river in front of her.

Michael grinned. "We've only seen a few this whole trip, and none of them came near us. We'll be fine." At least he hoped. He'd heard of big bull gators becoming aggressive toward humans, but after what happened in the creek earlier with Laurie, he didn't want her to get upset. They didn't need to end up in the water again.

He shifted forward and continued the trek toward the bay, one stroke at a time. The monotonous ribbon of green on both sides of him coupled with his exhausted body lulled him into a trance-like rhythm as he paddled.

Questions floated in and out of his mind. Was a Flamingo Cay police officer tied up in what happened? Had the killer found his partner's airboat? If so, how? And just how were they going to sneak into town and keep the girls protected?

"Michael."

Kyra's shout snapped him out of his daze. He peered toward her. The horror on her face alerted him to danger.

"Jaws," Laurie screamed while Amy waved her arm toward the left side of the boat.

A huge alligator came fast toward his kayak as though he were charging it in a territorial challenge. His mouth went dry. Michael stopped stroking the water so his craft was between the reptile and Kyra's. He raised his arm, and when the gator was within two feet, he reached out and brought his paddle down on its snout once. Then again.

The monstrous animal diverted its path, going behind the boat toward the bank. Michael fastened his gaze onto the alligator even when it scurried out of the river onto the shore. Without taking his eyes off the reptile, he said, "Everyone okay?"

"We're fine." Kyra's voice held strength in it. "But you shouldn't have risked getting so close to him. I could have shot at him and hopefully scared him away, or if I had to, kill him."

"You got your gun wet." He hadn't really thought his plan of action out other than to protect them.

"A Glock works even if it gets wet."

"Now you tell me." He looked at Amy, who stared at the animal on the bank, then Laurie, her face drained of all color. "Laurie, we're all right. Understand?"

For a long moment the teen, with her attention fixed on her lap, didn't say anything. Finally she nodded.

"Let's book it." Michael took his paddle and put all the power he could behind his strokes to take him as far away as possible from the rogue alligator.

Kyra kept up with him as they headed toward Egret Bay. Fifteen minutes later, they came to it.

Michael halted by the shore and scouted the area. "See anything suspicious?"

In the dim light of dusk Kyra shook her head. "Let's wait until dark and then keep close to the shoreline. We'll have to take it slow, but there will be some moonlight."

Michael gestured toward the sky. "I'm not so sure about that. Clouds are moving in. Maybe the storm is hitting early."

Two hours later, in the middle of a downpour, Kyra clambered out of the kayak at the old pier near Pelican Lane and tied it to the dock. Soon Michael and the girls joined her. He had a flashlight with him that shone on the gaping holes in the boards as they made their way to the path that led through the swampy area near their street. Thoughts of a hot shower urged her to go faster, but she knew the folly in that. The nearer they got to her house the more cautious they had to be.

Lightning flashed, illuminating the eerie darkness, followed almost immediately by a clap of thunder. Kyra flinched as the sound rumbled through the trees. Soaking wet, she trudged at the rear of the foursome toward her house. Rain had drenched them ever since they paddled halfway around Egret Bay to the canal opening. Although it had made their trip more difficult, she'd been glad for the cover of the storm that had rapidly moved into the area. During parts of the trip, she hadn't even been able to see three feet in front of her kayak. But that meant if anyone was waiting for them to return, he couldn't see them most likely. She was counting on that.

Lord, please help us to get home safely.

At the edge of the swamp, Michael paused, clicking off his flashlight. Kyra scanned the street and spied a patrol car in front of her house. She tensed. Friend or foe, and how would she know which?

"The police," Michael whispered against her ear. "How should we handle this?"

"You can't say anything to them," Amy said, her voice laden with fear.

"I'm not going to. But maybe Michael and I should go inside and see why they are at my house. If we don't, that will alert whoever is part of what's going on that something isn't right."

"Where do we go?" Quaking, Laurie hugged herself.

"My garage. We can get in on the side. You'll be out of the rain, and then when the officer leaves, I'll let you into the house." In the dark Kyra couldn't see the teen's face, but she dropped her arms to her sides.

"Do you think it's safe to go?" Michael asked.

"Let's go through the bushes over there—" Kyra pointed to thick foliage in the direction of the Gulf "—and go around the back close to the Pattersons' house, then through the hibiscus hedge. The garage door is right there."

She sensed Amy nod her head while Laurie squeaked out, "Okay."

Kyra withdrew her gun and held it up. "I want you all behind me. Amy and Laurie, then Michael. No talking, and stay in the shadows as much as possible. The rain should help."

Plunging into the vegetation to her left, Kyra forged ahead, determinedly ridding her mind of their encounters with a snake and alligator earlier that day. *The Lord is with me. I can do anything. Even walk in complete darkness through the swamp.*

Mud found its way into her tennis shoes and oozed between her toes. Branches slapped at her legs and arms. Mosquitoes buzzed her. She sloshed ahead, concentrating on what little she could see. In the distance she heard the waves crashing against the shore. Another slash of lightning illuminated her dark surroundings for a second, allowing her to get her bearing. Only a few more yards.

Near the Pattersons' yard her foot caught on a fallen limb. She started to go down and latched on to a small tree trunk close by. After steadying herself, she kept going, stopping for a moment to scour the terrain in front of her before emerging from the dense vegetation.

She felt as if she'd broken free from jail. Waiting

for the others, she stood guard, slowly making a full circle, squinting her eyes to see into the blackness. When Michael and the girls joined her, she covered the distance behind the neighbor's house and wedged between two hibiscus bushes to come out near the door to the garage at her family home. The key to the front door fit this one, too. She dug into her jean pocket, thankful she hadn't lost her keys when she'd gone into the creek.

Quickly she unlocked the side door and whispered, "Amy, Laurie, stay in here. Lock the door when I shut it. When it's safe, we'll come get you. Okay?"

"Yes," Amy said in a lowered voice and stepped into the garage, followed by Laurie.

When Kyra heard the click of the lock, she started around the house to the front. She let the rain rinse the mud off her clothes before she climbed the stairs to the porch and took off her tennis shoes. Then she fit her key into the lock and opened the door slowly, listening for people talking.

A deep baritone and Aunt Ellen's voice came from the great room in back. Not Gabe's. She knew how he sounded like a gruff bear. Who? Connors? Nichols? Tiptoeing into the foyer, she started to sneak toward the room when lights from another car coming into the driveway shone through the screen door as Michael turned to close it. Kyra halted and came back to Michael, peering outside to see who else had arrived.

Gabe ran through the rain to the porch. "Where have y'all been? I was about to send out a search party for y'all."

Kyra stepped between Michael and Gabe. "We went out looking for Amy and Laurie in the swamp. Did you all find anything?"

"I tried you on your cell. No answer." A frown marred Gabe's face.

"When I checked it a few hours ago, it was out of juice. I forgot in all the commotion last night to recharge my battery. Did something happen?"

Kyra heard footsteps coming from the great room and peeked around to see Aunt Ellen and Officer Connors join them.

Gabe shook his head. "We came up empty. Why did y'all go off by yourself?"

Kyra frantically searched for a reasonable answer to that question.

"I thought of another place Amy liked to go, and it was a good distance north of here. We left at dawn," Michael said.

"And you didn't bother telling me so I didn't send anyone that way?"

"Sorry, Gabe. Aunt Ellen knew we were out looking."

"Yeah, but no info where? You know how a

search works." Disappointment peppered each of Gabe's words.

"I thought you were covering the Manatee Creek area." Water dripping off him, Michael combed his fingers through his soaking-wet hair.

Kyra wanted to tell Gabe what was going on, but one glance at Michael's stony expression and she kept her mouth closed. She couldn't, though, erase the feeling she was betraying her mentor by not letting him in on the fact they had the girls.

"Chief, I'll leave you all here and head home. I expect we'll have another early morning."

Gabe gave Connors a nod while the officer passed him in the foyer and departed, closing the front door.

"Well, my goodness, y'all are wet. While you go get changed, I'll wipe up your mess in here and put some coffee on. It may be summer, but I imagine y'all are chilled from the rain. You look like drowned rats. What did you do—go swimming?" Aunt Ellen shooed Kyra and Michael toward the hallway.

"No, Auntie, we just got caught in a downpour."

Gabe shrugged out of his rain slicker, his sharp gaze glued to Kyra. "I'm surprised Ken's airboat didn't have any of these for our sudden thunderstorms that pop up at this time of year."

"Not that we knew of," she mumbled and made her way toward her bedroom.

With a change of clothes in his hand, Michael halted her halfway down the corridor and drew her close, bending his head toward her ear to whisper, "He knows something's up."

"You think? We should tell him we have Amy and Laurie."

"No." The word came out on a harsh rush of air. "I realize there's a slim chance it's Gabe, but it's a chance I can't take. Let's see what we can figure out tomorrow."

"If we come up empty, we need to reconsider bringing Gabe in on this. He knows this area better than most. He knows the law-enforcement officers in the county. It might not be one on his force. It could be a deputy, even the sheriff. For that matter, it could be a game warden. They police the Everglades."

"Do you have some blankets handy? I want to sneak out to the garage if you keep Gabe occupied. I'm sure the girls are cold and frightened."

Kyra peered behind her to make sure no one was there to see what she did, then she went to the linen closet at the end of the hall and took down two blankets. "Tell them to sit in my rental car. If they're tired, they can lie down in it. Also something to eat and drink if you can without Gabe seeing you."

With his free hand, he cupped her face and looked long and hard into her eyes. "I don't know what I would have done if you hadn't chosen this time to come back to Flamingo Cay. I'm so out of my element."

The touch of his fingers against her skin branded her. What they had gone through the past three days formed a bond between them that she'd never felt before and his caress only reinforced that connection. "Sorta like me trying to save someone who came into the E.R."

One corner of his mouth cocked up. "Yeah. I guess we each have our expertise."

"Wait five minutes in the bathroom before you go to the garage. I'll hurry and change and make sure to keep Gabe occupied."

He leaned toward her and gave her a light kiss on the lips, saying, "Thanks," then went into the bathroom behind him.

Leaving Kyra bereaved as though she'd been deprived of something wonderful. She wanted the kiss to go on. She wanted his touch to last. With a shake of her head, she hurried into her bedroom. What was he doing to her? He was her best friend in high school's kid brother. She had no business getting romantically involved, especially with someone who lived halfway across the country from her. So many reasons screamed for her to back off and quickly.

But as she shed her wet, dirty clothes and ran a wet washcloth over herself, then donned a clean pair of slacks and three-quarter-sleeve shirt to hide her cuts and bruises from her trek through the Everglades, she couldn't rid herself of the sensation she'd felt ever so briefly when his lips had brushed across hers.

As she passed the closed bathroom door, she tapped on it and kept going down the hall. When she entered the great room and glimpsed Aunt Ellen and Gabe sitting next to each other on the couch, heads close together, talking in low voices, she couldn't fathom her mentor being connected to the man who had killed Preston and his cousin and was now after Amy and Laurie—even her and Michael. But she would honor Michael's wishes and talk with a few friends she had in the FBI and the Florida state police.

"Kyra, are you all right?" her aunt asked from across the room, tiny grooves pleating her forehead.

Kyra forced a smile. "Fine, just tired." She crossed to a lounge chair and sat. "Gabe, I hope you can tell me you have some good news, some leads to follow."

"That's why I came over here. I just got news that Cherie woke up briefly but slipped back into unconsciousness after a few minutes. The doctor feels that she'll make it but might go in and out of consciousness over the next few days. Her body and mind were put through a horrible ordeal."

"So no one has talked to her?" Kyra tried to relax back in her lounger, but her muscles were bunched so tightly that it was impossible to get comfortable—not when the girls were hiding in the garage and the killer could be outside watching the house. Waiting for his chance to finish what he'd begun.

"What little Cherie said to the doctor didn't make sense. Something about a black snake. He didn't even feel she was aware of her surroundings."

"A black snake?" Kyra mumbled, picturing the python gliding through the water straight toward her, his tongue flicking, his eyes boring into her.

"Gabe—" Aunt Ellen put her hand on the police chief's arm, further pulling his attention to her "—don't mention snakes around Kyra. She doesn't fear a lot of things, but snakes head the list."

He laughed. "I certainly remember that. Once her dad and I found one in the yard and I never saw a child high-tail it into the house so fast. She locked every window and door and wouldn't let her father and me in until we had assured her we had gotten rid of the varmint."

"Hey, I was only nine at the time."

"Oh, dear, I forgot to put the coffee on." Aunt Ellen started to rise.

Kyra hopped up, waving her down. "I'll do it. You stay and entertain Gabe." She shot them a grin and strolled out of the room, glancing back at the doorway to make sure her aunt was occupying Gabe's full attention.

Aunt Ellen had forgotten all about her and the coffee as she shifted toward the police chief, two patches of pink highlighting her cheeks. "When are you going to take me out target practicing?"

A laugh escaped Kyra's mouth as she entered the kitchen, her gaze straying to the door that led to the garage. Her aunt was one of a kind. Tough as nails but every bit as feminine with her perfectly made-up face, manicured nails and stylish hairdo with probably tons of hair spray to keep it in place.

While she put a pot of coffee on to brew, Michael came up behind her and whispered, "They're fine. I think if I hadn't gone out to the garage when I did, they would have fallen asleep on the concrete floor. The blankets and granola bars were welcomed."

The caress of his breath as he spoke against her ear tickled her and flashed goose bumps down her length. She stepped forward a few inches, up against the counter, and shifted toward Michael. For a moment she couldn't think of a thing to say as she looked into his glimmering eyes. Finally she said the first thing that came to her mind, "The coffee should be—"

He tugged her flat up against him while winding his arms around her. His mouth settled on hers, further robbing her of any coherent thoughts. Instead she experienced a barrage of sensations from the shortness of breath to the warmth that suffused her whole body to the sinking feeling in the pit of her stomach.

When Michael ended the kiss, he still kept her locked in his embrace, plastered against him, the pounding of his heart flowing from his body into hers. He laid his forehead against hers, sucking in deep breaths.

"I've waited twenty years for that." The flow of his words over her lips tickled them.

"You thought of kissing me when you were thirteen?"

"Yep. You were my first crush. An older, mysterious woman."

"You saw me practically every day. There couldn't be anything mysterious about me."

"In my fantasy, there was."

"What about your teenage crush on Melissa?"

"She did take my mind off you for a while." He straightened, a twinkle in his eyes. "You know how fickle teenage boys can be." He winked and dropped his arms back to his side.

"My goodness, what has been keeping y'all?" Aunt Ellen scurried into the kitchen, making a bee-line for the coffeepot. "You two go in and entertain Gabe while I get this ready. I declare y'all are gonna need a chaperone before this is over with."

As Kyra and Michael walked from the room, she asked, "You heard her coming?"

"Yes. Why didn't you? Preoccupied?" Another wink accompanied those questions.

"You wish." She increased her pace and claimed the lounger across from where Michael took a seat. Thankful there were six or seven feet between them, Kyra concentrated on Gabe or at least tried to. "Was Connors here for any reason? He left so fast I didn't get to ask him."

"I didn't send him, but he was aware of how concerned and a little peeved I was at you for disappearing today. I'm getting up there in age and don't need any more stress, especially with all that's going on. Retirement is looking better and better."

"I'm sorry." Kyra stared at her lap, not wanting Gabe to realize how truly uncomfortable she was with the situation of not knowing whom to trust. When he discovered what they had done, he would be hurt, but she had to honor Michael's wishes on this. Amy was his sister.

Aunt Ellen came into the room carrying a tray with four mugs of coffee on it. She put it down on the table in front of the couch and passed the mugs to everyone. "It got awfully quiet in here. I was hoping you would have the case solved by now."

Gabe took a long sip of his drink, then placed the mug on the tray. "I wish we did, but it looks like it'll take a little longer. We expanded the search toward Manatee Creek, but still have some to do tomorrow. We haven't located the cabin, but the photo of the creek that was taken was found right before we had to return to town."

"Was anyone able to enhance the photo of the two men?" She brought her coffee to her lips and savored the brew.

"No, too blurry to tell who they are." Gabe pinned his gaze on Kyra and added, "I need to leave. Walk me to the door."

The quiet order conveyed the police chief's real intention. Kyra stood. "You look tired. You need to get some rest," she said to fill the charged silence between her and Gabe as they moved toward the foyer.

Out of earshot of Michael and Aunt Ellen, Gabe halted and pivoted toward her. "What's really going on?"

"We've been searching for Amy and Laurie. That advice I gave you is something I'm going to take for myself. Today has been long and exhausting, especially with the rain at the end. I felt like I was wearing ten pounds of clothes."

His penetrating gaze bore into her. "I trust you, Kyra. I asked you to help me because I do. I think there is more to this case. Preston's cousin has gang ties in Miami. The dagger is the gang's symbol, which means Preston was in the gang at one time.

From what I heard from the Miami police, though, he left it when he moved here."

"But you don't think he really did?"

Gabe shrugged. "Hard to tell. I've questioned the people he hung out with here in town. They have denied he was involved in anything in Flamingo Cay."

Kyra embraced Gabe. "We'll figure it out."

"If you ever want to go back into police work, I'm retiring. These past few days isn't normal. I promise most of the time it's quiet and peaceful."

She kissed his cheek. "What about Wilson?"

"He's still young and has some things to learn. You'd be a good teacher."

"I have a successful business I can't walk away from, but thanks for asking."

"Don't dismiss it. This little town has a lot to offer. Great doctors. Beautiful beaches. Delicious seafood." He grabbed the handle and opened the front door. "By the way, the bomb was detonated by a timer."

"We must have gotten there right after he placed it. I'm sure I saw something in the bush across the orchard."

"If only you two had arrived ten minutes earlier, we might have been able to catch this killer."

"By using a timer he hadn't intended to stay around waiting for us to show up to trap us, so why did he blow up the car? Something he didn't want us to find?"

"Maybe he was covering his tracks. He might have inspected the car and wanted to make sure he didn't leave any evidence behind that could be used against him. I doubt we'll be able to find anything left by him that could incriminate him. The car was burned pretty bad."

"Could be. Which means he's in the system somewhere probably."

"Good night. Get some rest, Kyra. I figure tomorrow will be another long day."

"You, too. This town needs you."

After Gabe left, Kyra hurried back into the great room. "He's gone."

Michael was on his feet the second she came through the entrance and striding toward the kitchen. "I told Aunt Ellen what was going on."

"Goodness, those girls have to be scared out of their mind. I've got some cookies and milk that should make them feel better." Aunt Ellen trailed them into the kitchen and went to the refrigerator.

"Auntie, why don't you order a couple of pizzas instead? They haven't eaten much except what Michael and I brought them."

"Oh, sure. You're right." She crossed to the phone on the desk. "They can have the cookies for dessert. I'll need to go to the grocery store and stock up."

While Michael disappeared into the garage, Kyra paused and turned toward her aunt. "Not too much. We don't want anyone to think we're feeding an army."

"Kyra, you're so good at this spy stuff. Well, not exactly spy stuff, but you know what I mean." Aunt Ellen began punching in the number of the lone local pizza restaurant.

Half-asleep, the two teens staggered in from the garage, the blankets wrapped around them. Behind them, Michael shut the door and locked it. Both girls blinked at the brightness of the light in the kitchen, ducking their heads down.

"Aunt Ellen ordered some pizzas. While we wait for them, why don't you two take a shower, and I'll find something for you to change into."

"Tomorrow I'll go back to our house and get some clothes for both of you." Michael pulled Amy into his arms. "I'm just glad you're here in one piece."

His sister leaned back and looked up into his face. "What if he finds us here?"

Michael started to say something but Kyra stepped toward the girls. "I'm not going to kid you. He might. But this place has a good alarm system and my business is protecting people. We'll keep the blinds pulled, all windows and doors locked, and we're going to work real hard to figure out what's going on and stop this guy before he can do anything else."

"Take a shower. Then we'll eat and discuss what happened." Michael rubbed his hands up and down Amy's upper arms.

Aunt Ellen rose from the desk, retrieving her gun from the large pocket of her dress. "No one is going to hurt you in my house."

Wild-eyed, Laurie glanced from Auntie's gun to Kyra's in its holster at her waist. "I need to let Mom know I'm all right. She doesn't know where I went. I didn't even have time to leave her a message. Can I at least call her?"

Kyra settled her arm along her shoulders. She and Michael had decided to wait to tell Laurie about her mother until she was back at the house. Kyra wished she didn't have to give this news to an already distraught girl. "She isn't at home. Your mom was hurt and is in the hospital, but she'll be all right."

Tears welled into Laurie's eyes. "Hurt? How?"

"The guy who's after you two beat her up."

"Because of me." The teen's legs gave out, and she would have sank to the floor if Kyra hadn't supported her weight. She helped the girl to a chair nearby.

"How bad?" Laurie asked, wet tracks streaking down her cheeks.

Kyra knelt in front of the teenager while Amy

clasped her friend's shoulder. "Pretty bad, but the doctor said she'll recover with time. Right now she is being guarded at the hospital so no one can get to her and harm her anymore."

"Can I talk to her?" Laurie swiped her forefingers across her cheeks, but the tears continued to fall.

Kyra grasped the girl's hands, waiting for her full attention. "She's sleeping a lot, which is what her body needs. We can't take the risk right now of letting anyone know you all are here. But as soon as I think it's safe, you can. Okay?"

Laurie nodded.

"We'll get him, Laurie. For Preston, Tyler and your mom." Amy's gaze latched on to Kyra.

The determination Kyra glimpsed in her blue depths spoke of a person who had done a lot of growing up in the past few days.

An hour later in the great room, Kyra gathered the empty boxes of pizza and headed for the kitchen. "Does anyone want anything else?"

"We're good." Michael sat next to his sister on the couch while Laurie was on the other side of Amy.

Kyra stacked the three empty boxes on the kitchen table, refilled her coffee, then hurried back into the great room. She and Michael had decided not to talk about the case until after everyone had eaten and gotten a second wind.

Aunt Ellen rose from the lounge chair. "I'm gonna leave y'all to talk. I'm changing the sheets on Kyra's bed so you two girls can share it. Please finish those cookies tonight if you're still hungry. I can always bake more tomorrow. Good night."

"Where are you sleeping?" Amy asked Kyra as her aunt left the room.

"With Auntie. Your brother will be in here on the couch."

After reaching for a chocolate-chip cookie, Amy pulled her feet up on the couch and tucked them under her, leaning against Michael. "I think I can draw a picture of the man who came after us—" she glanced at Laurie "—with your help." Amy took a big bite of the sweet. Her eyes grew huge.

"You don't have to eat it," Kyra said with a laugh.

Amy finished chewing the bite. "Won't your aunt be hurt if we don't?"

"I'll dispose of them so she won't know. She means well but just doesn't get it when she cooks. She won't follow a recipe and puts ingredients in without measuring. She doesn't even own measuring cups and spoons. Some cooks might be able to get away with doing that, but my aunt isn't one of them."

Amy bent forward and set the partially eaten cookie on the plate.

Kyra scooted to the end of her chair, clasping her hands together, her elbows on her thighs. "Tell me what happened again from the beginning. Everything you can remember. Don't leave out any detail. You never know when it could be important."

Amy peered at Laurie, who gave a slight nod. "Tyler wanted to go a little farther into the swamp than we've been going. Really explore the area." Amy shared another look with Laurie. "We think now Tyler was scouting the area for something or someone. Preston and him kept whispering between them."

"Do you think he was looking for the guy after you?"

Laurie shook her head. "He was as surprised as we were when we found the cabin. I don't think that was what he was looking for."

Kyra thought about the gang connection with Tyler—and even Preston. Maybe Tyler was here to do something for his gang. They might never know what it was he was looking for, but it wasn't important unless it pertained to the case. "Okay, you found this cabin that you thought would be deserted but it wasn't. How long were you all there before the man showed up?"

"Maybe ten minutes, tops." Amy lay her head on the back cushion, yawning.

"Where is this cabin?" Michael asked his sister.

"Due east about two hours, past Manatee Creek. We went by kayak. Even though I got turned around some, especially when we fled, I think I can find it again. Preston has been going into the Everglades a lot, even more than I do. He seemed to know about certain places more than me."

Was Preston helping his cousin somehow? Was what Tyler looking for connected in some way to the killer? "We might check out the cabin, but I seriously doubt anyone is there now. It has been compromised. He wouldn't have stuck around."

"The guys wanted to check the place out. I didn't think it would harm anything so I agreed."

Laurie frowned. "I wanted to leave. The place gave me the creeps."

Amy glanced at her friend. "I wish we had. Then maybe Preston and Tyler might not have taken the money."

Kyra straightened. "Money? What money?"

"There was a lot of money in a duffel bag. I mean, a *lot*." Massaging the side of her temple, Amy leaned forward, putting her feet on the floor. "Preston and Tyler each took about five thousand and there was still thousands left. The killer would have had to count it to know any was missing. Preston and Tyler took a little from each bundle of cash so the same number of bundles were there."

"Dr. Hunt, we begged the boys not to take the

money. They didn't think the person would miss it," Laurie said.

"So you think it's the missing money that made the man come after you all and kill Preston and Tyler?" Kyra realized people murdered for a lot less, but she had a feeling more than that was going on here.

"Yes, at least at first before he got the money back."

"What do you mean he got the money back?" Kyra asked.

"The man from the cabin found my cell and used it to text Preston. He told Preston to return the money he and his friends stole from him or we would regret it. No questions asked if Preston left it at the Pattersons' house. He knew all of our names."

"Even Tyler's?" Kyra leaned back in her chair.

Amy nodded.

Kyra glanced at Michael. "This reinforces the idea someone is helping him in the area. Gabe didn't know who Tyler was until Wilson tracked down the young man and found out he was Preston's cousin."

"So why did this man have thousands of dollars in a duffel bag in the middle of the Glades?" Michael kneaded his right shoulder.

"That's what Laurie and I have been asking

ourselves. We think he is being paid to do something bad." Amy sat forward.

"Why do you say that?" Kyra rose, restlessness zipping through her, tingling her nerve endings.

"Because of what else was in the duffel bag." Amy locked gazes with Kyra. "There were floor plans and a map of some place."

"Do you know where?" Kyra gripped the back of the lounge chair.

"There wasn't a name on the drawing."

"It was bigger than a house. A good-size building," Laurie chimed in.

Amy snapped her fingers. "Yes, and the little squares that I guess were rooms had numbers on them. Maybe an office building."

Laurie twisted her mouth into a thoughtful countenance. "Or hotel. Not everything was labeled, so it was hard to tell. I didn't get a good look at it."

"I did while Preston and Tyler were taking the money. I think I could recreate the plans." Amy closed her eyes for a moment, now rubbing her forehead.

"Are you all right?" Michael asked.

"I've got a headache. That's all."

"Me, too." Laurie's eyebrows dipped downward.

Michael pointed to their still half-full water glasses. "Both of you need to drink a lot of liquid. You might have been surrounded by water in the swamp, but that doesn't help you when you're thirsty. You're both dehydrated most likely."

As the teenage girls drank some water, Kyra walked to the picture window overlooking the beach and cracked the blind to peer out into the darkness. Nothing stirred except the branches of the palm trees as the light breeze caught them. She turned toward the trio. "What happened after the guys took the money?"

"I was looking out the broken glass pane in front and saw two men coming toward the cabin. I told Amy, Preston and Tyler we had to get out of there." Laurie shuddered.

"While the guys were putting the bundles of cash and the plans back in the bag the way they found them, I came over to Laurie to see who she was talking about. She looked scared."

"Because I was. Did you see that dark-haired man? That snake on his arm?"

"A tattoo or real?" Kyra remembered Cherie talking about a black snake getting her.

Another shiver wiggled down Laurie's length. "Not real, thankfully. But the man was wearing a sleeveless T-shirt and one arm had a big ugly black snake halfway down it."

"It covered him from the top by his shoulder to his elbow. His hair was long and pulled back in a ponytail. But what frightened me was his voice. Chilling. Raspy."

"Yeah, and he had a foreign accent. Spanish. Or Italian."

Amy exchanged a look with Laurie. "It was Spanish. He and the other, thin man slipped between Spanish and English."

"Could you hear what he was saying, Amy?" Kyra's fingers dug into the back cushion of the lounger so hard they cramped up. She loosened them and shook them.

"I've only had one year of Spanish, so I'm not very good, but I understood some of it. He was arguing with the other man about some job. He was questioning the thin man about his police contact having everything covered. His protection better be in place if they wanted the job done by Friday." Amy replaced her glass on the coffee table after drinking all the water.

"Did he see or hear you all?" Kyra tapped down her excitement at the leads the girls were giving her. There was still so much they didn't know, and if something was going to happen by Friday, which was two days away, time was running out on figuring out what was going down in Flamingo Cay or nearby.

"I didn't think so. When the thin man left, the other guy watched him for a minute, then started for the cabin. We had to hurry, but we were real quiet as we snuck out the back door. Laurie tripped over a stool but caught it before it crashed to the floor."

Something alerted the dark-haired man that someone had been in the cabin. What? "Do you think anything was out of place when you left? Maybe the stool in your haste to leave?"

Laurie shook her head. "I made sure to put it back exactly the way it was."

"So he didn't follow you from the cabin?"

"No, not that we knew, but the second we were away from the clearing, we ran as fast as we could to our kayaks and got out of there." Amy lowered her head, twisting her hands together in her lap. "That must have been when my phone fell out of my pocket. I got stuck in some mud for a few seconds and went down."

"We may never know how the man with the snake tattoo found your phone or discovered you all were in the cabin unless he tells us." As a police detective there were cases like that where she and her partner never knew all the details even when they caught the perpetrator. Very frustrating.

"I hope I never see that guy again." Amy hugged her arms across her chest.

"How did you end up at the Pattersons' house Monday morning? What happened there?" Kyra asked, picturing the young man staggering out of the hibiscus hedge onto the beach and collapsing into the sand.

"Michael had already left to deliver the baby when Preston called my house that night to have me meet him at the Pattersons'. He sounded different, but I just thought he was tired. I didn't get much sleep thinking about the money and the man. Later—" Amy glanced at Laurie "—I found out Tyler tried calling Laurie to come to the Pattersons', but she didn't answer. It was a setup. The dark-haired man forced the guys to call when they came to return the money." Amy lowered her head, entwining her fingers together. "He never intended to let Preston and Tyler go free." She raised her chin, her eyes shiny with unshed tears. "He wanted all of us there so he could kill us. We saw something at that cabin he didn't want us telling anyone."

"Or the fact you can ID the two guys, the one with the tattoo and the thin man. You said you think you can draw the dark-haired man. I'd like you to do what you can tonight, then look at it again when you've gotten a good night's sleep. And if you can draw the other man, great."

"Who is skullandcrossbones?" Kyra glanced at Laurie. "Was it you?"

Amy's friend nodded. "We set up an account under a false name."

Kyra thought about the fact Gabe said there was a second set of large footprints near the Pattersons' house. Maybe the thin man? Or the protection the killer talked about? She pushed to her feet and covered the distance to the desk, where she grabbed a few sheets of blank paper and a pencil. "Do what you can, Amy. Laurie, if you'd give her any insight into what you saw, that might help, too. The more accurate the drawing the better chance we have of finding who the guy is."

"How about the plans in the duffel bag?" Amy took the paper and pencil and sat on the floor by the coffee table with Laurie next to her.

"Do what you can tonight? I know you're both tired." Kyra nodded as Laurie tried to stifle a yawn.

Michael took the plates and glasses. "I'll get you some more water." Snatching Kyra's attention, he nodded his head toward the kitchen.

Kyra trailed him into the room. "What's up?"

"The more I think about it I don't think it's safe to stay here."

"I agree. We could head for Naples. Stay in a hotel."

"I've got a better idea. I have a college friend who now lives on Marco Island. He has some rental property, and I think we could get something from him."

"Do you trust him?"

"Yes. He doesn't have any ties to the Flamingo Cay area. He grew up in Panama City. We've kept in touch over the years since college. Although he doesn't live far from here, we've both been so busy we haven't had a chance to get together yet since I came back to Florida."

"Does anyone know about him here?"

"No."

"When this is over, you should take some time for yourself. When I was working for the police, I didn't have a life outside my job. Even though starting my business has been time-consuming, I've managed to carve some time for leisure with friends." But not nearly enough, she realized. Her near brushes with death had emphasized that to her.

Michael sent her a tired smile. "I'm realizing that. You can't drown herself in work in order to avoid your problems. It might work for a while but not long. The problem is still there to be solved."

The urge to put her arms around him and hold him close inundated her. She'd done her fair share of avoiding problems until they hit her in the face and demanded attention. "I think we need to leave tonight after midnight."

"How? Our cars can be traced and don't rental cars have GPS?"

"Yes, I'm sure the one I have does." A movement out of the corner of her eye caused Kyra to swing around toward the entrance into the dining room.

Laurie, pale, hugging her arms to her chest, stood in the doorway. "We could use Mom's car."

"The white one sitting in the driveway? I think people would notice it was gone," Kyra said.

"No, the one she inherited from her mother when

she died last year. It's old but it runs and it's sitting in the garage. Not many people know about it. She brought it home and parked it in the garage. She started it every once in a while to keep the battery charged, but she hasn't driven it around town."

"Perfect." Kyra closed the distance between her and Laurie. "I'll go get it and bring back some clothes for you and Amy. You two look about the same size." She glanced at Michael. "I'd prefer you not go back to your house. When I get the car, I can call and you can escort the girls and Aunt Ellen to Bay Shore Drive via the beach where I will pick you all up. We should assume someone might be watching our houses here on Pelican Lane. When I sneak out, I'll tell you the best way to leave here when I call. It shouldn't take me more than thirty minutes to get to Laurie's on foot."

"When I watched these kinds of things in a movie, I never thought I would ever be doing something like this." Michael's mouth thinned into a frown.

"No one ever does." Kyra peered back at Laurie. "Do you have a key to your house?"

The teen dug into her jean shorts pocket, pulled a set of keys from it and offered them to Kyra. "This is it. The key to the car is on a peg in the utility room that leads to the garage."

"Thanks. You and Amy need to be ready to leave here in an hour."

"We'll finish what we can on the drawings." Laurie unfolded her arms and inhaled a deep breath. "We'll be ready."

Kyra smiled. "I know you two will be."

When Amy's friend left the kitchen with two glasses of water, which was why she'd come into the room, Kyra faced Michael. "I'll let Aunt Ellen know what we'll be doing, then I'll pull my things together and leave."

"No, you won't."

ELEVEN

"What do you mean I won't?" Kyra scrunched her forehead and squared her shoulders.

"Because I'm going to Laurie's to get the car."

"No, too dangerous."

In two steps he came within inches of her and bent toward her, close to her ear. "First, I know this town better than you do and know the shortest way to get to her house. Second and most important, I need you to stay here and do what you do best—protect. So between the two jobs, I'm better suited to get the car. Nothing can happen to Amy, Laurie or your aunt. Agreed?"

The quiet intensity in his words bombarded Kyra. She couldn't deny his logic, and yet she didn't want to send him out possibly to be murdered by the killer or his cohorts. The girls had answers to what might be going down in two days. They had to be protected at all costs. "Aunt Ellen is here to help you."

"No, it's not negotiable. I'm going to Laurie's."

He drew back, his expression set in determination, a nerve in his cheek twitching. "If it makes you feel any better, I was on the boxing team in college, and when I did go to the movies, I always watched action ones."

"Now I feel one hundred percent better. By all means you should go."

He grinned. "I knew you would see it my way."

Kyra fisted her hands at her waist. "In case you haven't figured it out I was being sarcastic."

He tweaked her nose with the tip of his forefinger. "That message came across loud and clear, and I'm ignoring it." He held his palm out flat. "Keys, please. I need to pack my things and leave."

Grumbling under her breath about stubborn men, Kyra gave him what he wanted, then stalked toward the hallway. He peered into the great room and swallowed several times. Now he had to tell Amy what he was doing. He didn't look forward to that and half thought about just going, but his sister deserved more than that.

When he entered the room, Amy glanced up and smiled. "This is coming along better than I thought. All those art lessons Ginny paid for are finally being used. Wanna see?" She held up the paper that revealed a dark-headed man with his hair pulled back in a ponytail, close-set eyes as black as his hair, several days' growth of a beard and thin lips. "And this is the snake on his right arm." She pointed to another drawing on the coffee table.

"Great." Crossing to his gym bag, he began stuffing his few belongings on the desk into it, which took all of half a minute. Then he pivoted, Amy's attention fixed on him.

"Laurie told me about what Kyra is gonna do."

Amy's friend leaped to her feet and muttered, "I'll get our stuff from the dryer. Our clothes should be dry by now."

After Laurie scurried from the great room, Michael leaned back against the desk and fortified himself with a gulp of air that didn't nearly fill his lungs enough. "There's been a change of plans. I'm going to Laurie's instead of Kyra."

Amy dropped the pencil and bolted to her feet. "You can't. You could get killed."

"I'm not going to get killed." He hoped. His life was in the Lord's hands. "This is the only way we should do it. Kyra needs to stay here and make sure you all are safe. I don't think we convinced Gabe we aren't up to something."

"You think the police chief is the dirty cop?"

"I don't know, so we have to assume everyone is until we can prove otherwise. Even if he wasn't, he trusts his men and might say something to one of them. Either way we need to get out of here before someone comes looking." He shoved himself off the desk and strode to Amy, taking her into his embrace. "I'll be all right. And after this is all over with, you and I need to sit down and have a good long talk. Start over fresh. A deal?"

She nodded against his chest and tightened her arms around him. When she stepped back, her eyes shone with tears. "Just come back. Please."

"He will," Kyra said from the entrance into the great room.

Michael swept around. The urge to hold her and never let go engulfed him in needs he'd decided he couldn't afford after Sarah died. A knot jammed his throat. Her look sliced through his defenses.

Amy kissed Michael on the cheek then hurried toward the kitchen. "Laurie needs my help."

"Because if you don't come back okay, I'll..." Kyra's thick voice faded into the sudden silence that gripped the room. She lowered her head while curling and uncurling her hands at her sides.

He took four steps and tugged her toward him. "There is nothing that will keep me away. I know those are just empty words, but I believe every one of them. We're going to make it away from Flamingo Cay and figure out what's going on. Stop what's planned for Friday and catch the bad guys. Just like in the movies." Cupping her face, he stared into her golden-brown eyes, which reminded him of dark honey. "Then you and I need to talk."

Before she said anything, he crushed his mouth into hers, taking it in a deep, soul-giving kiss.

Then he backed away or he would never want to leave her embrace. "Be ready to go in forty-five minutes." Swiveling, he made his way toward the garage and its side door.

Michael turned Laurie's key in the back door and eased it open. The hinges squeaked and the sound seemed to echo through the still night. His heart pumped the blood through his body at a dizzying speed. An owl hooted in a nearby tree, and he jerked, every muscle stiffening. In the distance a dog began to bark.

He threw a glance over his shoulder before entering the house. Darkness greeted his inspection of the backyard. He didn't think anyone had followed him from Kyra's—at least he hoped not. He shut the door and the click of the latch thundered through his mind as though he were announcing to the world he was sneaking into Laurie's house.

His one consolation was that at least his sister was safe. Kyra knew what she was doing even if he wasn't sure he did. He moved to the windows and made certain the blinds were pulled before he switched on his flashlight.

Now to grab some clothes for Laurie, then the car, and get out of here. Urgency propelled him forward, and he muted his flashlight until the curtains were closed as he moved through the place to Laurie's bedroom. After stuffing some items into a backpack he found in the disarray scattered all over the teen's floor, he started back down the hallway. A noise stopped him dead in his tracks.

"I tried to give Michael my gun, but he wouldn't take it." Aunt Ellen paced the kitchen. "Shouldn't he be calling by now?"

Kyra checked her watch for the tenth time in the past thirty minutes. "No. He'd just be getting to Laurie's about now. Auntie, sit. You're making me nervous, and the girls don't need to see you like this."

Aunt Ellen raked her fingers through her hair. Stray strands stuck out at odd angles from the perfectly set coiffure. "Something's not right. I can feel it. Call him."

"We need to give him more time."

"Okay. Five minutes. My feelings are usually right. Well, except that time your dad was perfectly fine out on the boat. He didn't appreciate me sending the coast guard out looking for him."

Kyra chuckled in spite of the huge knot twisting her stomach. Her father had been so upset with his sister he had called Kyra in Dallas and ranted over the phone for an hour about Auntie before he calmed down enough. Although only a moment had passed, she glanced at her watch again. Twenty-five minutes after midnight. "Have you got everything you need for a few days?"

"I was packed a couple of minutes after you told me to be. This is all I need." Her aunt patted the pocket that held her gun.

"Auntie, I'm getting kinda worried about you. Where is this coming from?" She waved her hand toward her aunt's hidden weapon.

"Child, I'm sure you aren't oblivious to all the violence in this world. A person has to be prepared, especially one who lives by herself."

The doorbell chiming resonated through the house. Kyra froze. Amy and Laurie raced into the kitchen.

Amy skidded to a halt. "Someone's here. That wouldn't be Michael, would it?"

Kyra strode toward the foyer.

"Don't answer it," Laurie whispered, grabbing her arm. "It could be the bad guys."

"I won't know who it is until I look, and I seriously doubt the bad guys would announce themselves." Kyra gently tugged herself free and resumed her trek toward the front door. "Auntie, keep an eye out back, please."

"Will do. A diversion would be just what they would do. You girls go hide in the bathroom."

The sound of scurrying feet followed Kyra into

the foyer. When she heard a door shut down the hallway, she peered out the peephole.

Officer Wilson stood in the glow of the porch light.

Footsteps. In the kitchen.

Michael clicked off the flashlight and ducked into the nearest bedroom—where they'd found Cherie. The thought of her being left beaten, on the edge of death, seized Michael's mind, stealing his next breath. His chest ached as he put his hands out to feel where he was. His right one came into contact with a dresser. He trailed its length. If he remembered correctly, the closet was a few feet from it.

He finally took a deep gulp of air when he found the closet door ajar. He slipped inside and hid behind the dresses. Trying to calm the hammering of his heart, he listened for any noise coming from the hallway.

Nothing.

Had he imagined footsteps in the kitchen?

Indecision nipped at his resolve to stay where he was until he knew for sure. Whoever it was could have gone in the other direction.

If there was anyone else in the house.

Doubts welded with his indecision. What would Kyra do?

Forget that. He wasn't Kyra. She knew what she was doing. She'd have a gun and confront the person. He was empty-handed, except for the flashlight.

He stepped from behind the clothes as his cell vibrated in his pocket and the bedroom light came on.

Kyra's hand went to the top of her Glock in her holster as she backed away to open the door. When she swung it wide, her arm slipped to her side, near her gun. Every nerve settled into an alert mode. Her blood scorched a path through her body, sending her pulse rate up.

"It's after midnight. Is something wrong?" Kyra swallowed to coat her dry throat.

Wilson touched the brim of his hat. "I saw the lights on and thought I would check to make sure you all were all right. Chief asked me when I patrol tonight to come by every hour."

"He did?"

"With all that's happened, he's worried. I don't blame him. Something bad is going down here."

"Aunt Ellen and I are fine. We've been up trying to figure out what's going on but no luck."

"How about Dr. Hunt? He didn't go back to his house alone, did he?"

"No, he's asleep. Exhausted. These past days have been hard on him with his sister gone."

"Don't blame him. I have a younger sister in college who's given my parents a few gray hairs."

"Tell Gabe I've got him on speed dial and not to worry."

"I'll pass that message along—tomorrow morning." He nodded and turned to leave. "Good night."

A muffled pop then a faint thud sounded. The wood near Kyra's right cheek splintered.

"What are ya doing in here?" Connors asked, his gun drawn, aimed at Michael's chest.

His wide gaze riveted to the barrel. Connors was the bad cop?

"Dr. Hunt?"

Michael blinked, trying to think of some excuse he could give for being in the Carsons' house. Nothing came to mind. "Why are you here?"

"A neighbor saw a light on in here. He was sure the killer had come back and was going to murder everyone on the street in their bed."

Michael's cell vibrated again. He stared down at his jean pocket.

"Aren't ya going to answer your phone?"

"Sure." He slid his hand in and clasped the cell. When he brought it to his ear, he said, "Hi, Kyra. What do you need?"

"This isn't Kyra," Amy said in a loud whisper.

"Yes, I understand." He gave Officer Connors a grin.

"What's going on, Michael? Are you all right?" Amy asked.

"Maybe."

"We aren't. A cop came to the door and…"

Michael started to respond to his sister, aware of Connors's full attention tracking his every move, but Amy gasped and cried out, "Something is wrong."

"I'll be right there." Michael hung up and dropped the phone in his pocket. "I need to get to Kyra's."

"No, you don't. You aren't going anywhere."

A bullet struck the wooden door frame. Kyra ducked back against the wall while Wilson dived into the foyer and slammed the door shut with a kick. She drew her Glock as Wilson rolled over and leaped to his feet.

"Where's your aunt and Dr. Hunt? We need to get them away from the windows."

"I'm right here." Aunt Ellen appeared in the foyer from the great room, her hands stuffed into her pockets.

"Where's the doctor?" Wilson peered behind her aunt.

"He's not here." Kyra moved into the kitchen, flipping the light off then striding to the bay window that faced the street and peeking out the blind.

Another shot, coming from across the road where dense vegetation grew, took out the porch light, throwing the yard into darkness. The assailant was using a silencer—like Monday morning in the Pattersons' house. Adrenaline whipped through her system. Her fingers locked about her gun, her attention totally focused on the area where the assailant was positioned.

"Where is Dr. Hunt?" Wilson came up behind her.

Kyra tensed, throwing him a glance. "He had an errand to run."

"At midnight?"

"An emergency."

"When's he gonna be back?"

"Don't know. I couldn't stop him. He insisted on leaving." The feeling she was being interrogated swept through her. An alarm clanged in her mind. She shifted toward the officer and saw in the light streaming from the foyer that he pointed his weapon at her chest, his back against the wall.

"Get over there with your niece," Wilson said to Aunt Ellen. When she moved slowly, he motioned with his gun. "Now!"

"What's going on?" Kyra asked, even though she was sure this was the law-enforcement officer Amy overheard the killer mentioning. She didn't want him to think she knew about the connection.

She needed to protect Amy and Laurie and didn't want to give the impression she'd talked to either girl.

"You all are getting too nosy. You need to be stopped." Wilson switched on the overhead light. "I know about your gun in your pocket, Ms. Morgan. Remove it slowly and place it on the table. Then it's your turn, Kyra. If you make one false move, I'll kill your aunt."

He was going to kill them anyway, but she wasn't going to point that out to him. She would stall for time and try to come up with a way to get everyone out alive. "Who's outside?"

Wilson grinned. "Someone to make sure no one disturbs me this time."

"This time? Are you the one who attacked me on the beach?"

The gleam in his eyes answered her question, clinching their fate.

"What do you mean I can't leave?" Michael asked Officer Connors standing in Cherie Carson's bedroom, blood from the woman still staining the carpet.

"I need to call the chief. You broke into this house. In Florida that's against the law."

"No, I didn't. I have a key."

One of Connors' eyebrows arched. "Where did ya get a key?"

Michael's mind went blank. Slowly his dilemma leaked into his thoughts. If he told Connors, that would expose Amy and Laurie. If he didn't...

His cell went off again.

"I need to get this."

"Fine." The officer lowered his gun but didn't holster it.

"Michael, a cop is holding Kyra and her aunt at gunpoint in the kitchen."

"Who?"

"I'm not sure. It isn't the police chief. I know his voice. I peeked out when I heard the porch light being shot at right outside the bathroom window. When I couldn't see anything in the hall, I snuck to the foyer and overheard him in the kitchen telling Kyra and her aunt to put their guns on the table. Didn't you say Kyra was helping the chief with the murders? Then why would the cop in the kitchen do that unless he was helping the killer?"

"Where are you now?"

"Still in the bathroom."

"Can you get to a closet? If he sees the bathroom door closed, he might wonder why. I don't want him getting curious."

"I don't think he knows we're here."

"Keep it that way. If you don't think you can move to a bedroom, hide in the bathtub and pull the shower curtain."

"I'm scared."

The fear in his sister's voice highlighted the impotency he felt at the moment. "So am I. Love you."

"Ditto."

When Amy hung up, Michael wanted to get her back on the line and keep the connection open, but he knew that wasn't a good idea. She didn't need to be talking to him. She needed to find a hiding place. He lifted his gaze to Connors's troubled one. "Call Gabe. We've got a serious problem."

"We know that Laurie's cell phone was used to contact Michael Hunt. We know you two went into the swamp on Ken's airboat and left it in a creek. Where did you go? Why didn't you come back to that boat?"

"So you were there?"

"Not me."

Keep him talking. "How did the killer know where we went? We were careful to make sure no one was following us." Going fast in the airboat made that easier than if they had been in a kayak.

"Once Michael borrowed his partner's boat, I decided to put a GPS tracker on it in case he decided to do it again. I needed to keep tabs on where you all went."

"And then you alerted the killer. Why?"

"Simple. Lots of money. I have no intention of staying in this backwater town and growing old like Gabe. I have plans that require money." Wilson stepped to the table and took first one gun then the other and tucked both of them in his waistband. "Where are the girls?"

"Amy and Laurie? I don't know. Don't you think if we did we would have let Gabe know?" A glimpse of Amy peering around the corner into the foyer caught Kyra's attention through the kitchen doorway. She quickly swept her gaze away so Wilson wouldn't see any reaction on her face.

"Where did you and Michael go?"

"Searching for the girls, but we came up empty-handed. I don't know why you think otherwise." Kyra forced a bravado into her voice while staring down the barrel of a gun.

Both eyebrows shot up. "Why did you leave the airboat tied up there? Where did you go from there?"

"We used a kayak to explore some of the creeks that were impassable with an airboat. We didn't find them, though."

"I don't buy that. Are they here?"

She stared into his ice-gray eyes and said without hesitation, "No."

He laughed, a chilling sound. "Forgive me if I don't take your word for it. You two move into the foyer and stand at the entrance to the bedroom hallway."

As Kyra did as ordered, she exchanged glances

with Aunt Ellen. A calm expression met her perusal. *Lord, this is in Your hands.*

"Stop right there and turn around."

Kyra faced Wilson.

"Amy. Laurie. If you don't come out now, I will shoot first Kyra then Ellen. Don't make me come looking for you." He screwed a silencer on his gun.

Peace took hold of Kyra. She was in the best hands. Even when she glimpsed the coldness in Wilson's eyes, she clung to her composure.

"I'll give you to the count of three. One. Two. Three." Wilson pulled the trigger back and released it.

TWELVE

Gabe met Michael and Connors at the intersection of Pelican Lane and Bay Shore Drive, pulling across the road to block any traffic from turning onto Michael's street. "Have you heard anything?"

"Nope, Chief. It's been quiet." Connors closed his car door.

Michael stared at Kyra's house, at the darkness surrounding it. "Amy told me someone shot at the porch light. It's off." His gut roiled at the implication.

"You and I will have a talk later when we get everyone out safely. This should never have happened." His clipped words and fierce expression emphasized the police chief's anger.

And at the moment Michael couldn't blame him. He was mad at himself for not being at the house to stop what was happening inside. Thoughts of assault victims brought into the E.R. paraded across his mind, leaving him weak-kneed. He clutched the side of the car and leaned into it for support.

Was he going to be involved in the death of another woman he cared about? He couldn't lose Amy or Kyra.

"Amy said a cop was in the house with them, holding a gun on Ellen and Kyra. Where's his patrol car? Who is it? Are all your officers accounted for?"

"No. I can't raise Wilson. He isn't answering. The sheriff and some of his deputies are on the way. We should wait for them."

"We don't have time to wait. Four women's lives are at stake," Michael said as Nichols came to a stop in his personal car. The off-duty cop hopped out, dressed in jeans and a T-shirt but with his badge on and his holster with his weapon at his waist.

Gabe walked to his two officers and conferred with them in low tones, then they each went to the trunks of the patrol cars and donned their protective gear.

When the police chief paused in front of Michael, he said, "We're going in to check the situation out. See if we can find out what is going on in the house. Let the sheriff know what's happening, but you are not under any circumstances to come down the street or I will personally throw you in jail with great pleasure. Let me and my men handle this. You stay back here in the car." Gabe glared at Michael. "Understood?"

He nodded.

As Connors and Nichols moved down the street, Gabe took a few steps then glanced back and waited for Michael to climb into the patrol car.

Gabe and his officers slowly and cautiously made their way to Kyra's house. The endless seconds ticked by while Michael stayed put.

Father, protect them.

The wham from the weapon resonated through the foyer. Rigid, Kyra waited for the impact of the bullet to rip through her. It embedded itself into the wooden flooring right next to her foot. Her heartbeat momentarily slowed then revved up to a rapid pace. She fisted her hands.

"Stop. Stop. We're here." Crying, Amy clasped Laurie in the hallway by Kyra's bedroom, both girls quaking.

Wilson glanced toward the teens for a second then immediately returned his attention to Kyra and her aunt. "Get over here. You've caused me a lot of problems."

Amy and Laurie trudged toward the officer, their shoulders hunched. The look in their eyes conveyed fear but also rage. Kyra prayed they didn't try and do something stupid.

"Let's all go into there—" he waved his free hand toward the great room "—and have a little chat. On the couch. All of you."

Kyra sat on one end while Aunt Ellen took up the other with the two girls sandwiched between them. Kyra grasped Amy's hand. Michael's sister slanted a look toward her, her fear having completely replaced the anger in her expression.

Wilson stood in front of the coffee table, his glance taking in the sketches on it. "Who knows about him?"

Although he didn't explain whom he was talking about, it was obvious he was referring to the man in Amy's drawing. Kyra tightened her fingers around Amy's and said, "No one. We just got here and haven't had a chance yet to talk to anyone else."

"You didn't say anything to Gabe earlier this evening when he was here?" Wilson's gaze cut into her.

"No."

"I don't believe you." He skirted the table and hovered over Kyra. "Do I have to make an example out of you or maybe one of the girls to get a straight answer? Who else knows about him?"

Kyra assessed his intent and saw determination in his hard eyes. She released the breath she'd been holding. "Okay. Gabe knows and by now the state police and sheriff do."

A tic in his clamped jaw jerked. "I didn't hear anything before coming here."

"I asked him not to tell his officers. We knew one of you was crooked."

Thunder invaded his expression. He reached back and struck her across the face. "Liar."

Pain radiated outward from her jaw. Her vision blurred for a few seconds while a gong clanged through her head. The metallic taste of blood coated her tongue. She ignored all of that and lifted her chin. "It's only a matter of time before it's over for you. Amy warned Michael when she called him that a crooked cop was involved."

Gunfire from the street blasted through the air. Wilson pulled back, his gaze sweeping the room. He tossed two pairs of handcuffs to Kyra. "Put those cuffs on the girls and around those posts."

As she obeyed his orders, taking first Laurie then Amy to the support posts separating the dining room from the great room, another round of gunshots sounded. Her chest constricted. She fought to bring in a decent breath. Had Michael decided to come back to the house rather than wait for them on Bay Shore Drive? The assailant who had fired at the house earlier had a silencer. The shots she heard came from weapons without a silencer. The police?

"Hurry. You can move faster than that." Wilson's voice rose with each word he uttered.

He walked to the curtains and yanked the cord down then pitched it to Kyra. "Tie your aunt to the desk chair. I'm gonna check to make sure she's secure. If you don't do a good job, I'll take matters into my own hands." Agitation marked his tone and actions as he backed away from Kyra, keeping a lot of space between them.

As she twined the cord around her aunt's wrist, she whispered, "I'm so sorry."

"It's not your fault—"

"Shut up, you two. Now."

The whimpering cries from Amy and Laurie caused Wilson to swing toward them, aiming his gun. "Especially you all. You caused this."

While his attention was on the girls, Kyra poised herself to spring at the officer. *Now or never.*

The erupting sound of gunfire yanked Michael up straight in the patrol car. Were Kyra, Amy, Laurie and Ellen caught up in a shoot-out? What was going on?

He shoved open the door and stood, squinting to see down the lane with no streetlight. The only illumination came from a neighbor's security lamps. With the Pattersons' house dark and the porch light off at Kyra's, Michael couldn't tell what was going on very well.

Heart pounding, he closed the door and stepped a few feet away from the patrol car.

Another spattering of shots reverberated down the road and sent a shaft of fear down Michael's spine. That someone might be hurt enticed him a couple of more feet toward the far end of Pelican Lane. Then his promise to Gabe intruded, halting his progress.

Suddenly out of the dim shadows a thin man came right at him, gun in hand.

But before Kyra could launch herself at Wilson, he spun toward her. "Don't think it."

Settling back on the heels of her feet, she finished tying the cord around Aunt Ellen's hands, then took a pace back. Kyra glared at Wilson but clamped her lips together.

"Let's go." He waved the gun toward the kitchen. In the room, he pointed toward a chair at the table. "Sit. If you don't move, you might just live."

Kyra eased onto the hard surface and gripped the edge of the chair on either side of her. "It's over, Wilson."

He moved to the bay window, his gaze fixed on her except for a few seconds when he peeked outside. Anger deepened the grooves in his face. His Adam's apple bobbed as he turned his attention totally on her.

"You forget. I have you and the others."

"You know hostage situations never end well. You didn't kill the boys. You can make a deal and give the killer up."

The laugh that erupted from Wilson held a hint

of hysteria in it. "Yeah. People don't go against him and live. No thank you."

"You can go into protective custody."

A lone shot rang out—farther away than the recent volley of fire. The sound iced her blood. In the distance sirens blared, coming closer, but for some reason all Kyra could focus on was that single gunshot.

Frozen, Michael braced himself. The thin man, the one Amy told him had worked with the snake-tattoo guy, raised his gun and took aim.

The booming discharge of a pistol exploded in front of Michael. Every tense muscle waited for impact.

The thin man stepped forward, stumbled, his arm dropping to his side. Then down he went.

Stunned, Michael looked behind his assailant.

Gabe kept his gun trained on the man on the pavement as he strode toward him. "Are you okay?"

Michael wanted to pat his chest to make sure he wasn't just in shock but with a glance down, he only glimpsed his trembling hands. "Yeah. You?"

"I am, but Connors got shot. Can you take a look at him while I see to getting the others released?"

"You think Wilson has them?"

"Yes. His car is parked in the Pattersons' driveway out of sight from the road."

Michael walked to the thin man and knelt to

check to see if he was alive. The absence of a pulse only confirmed what he knew from the gaping hole in his upper back on the left side. He rose and continued his trek toward Connors sitting against Michael's car, which was parked out in front of Kyra's house.

He stayed in the shadows in case Wilson decided to take a shot at him. When he reached his car, he paused at Connors's side. "Where are you hit?"

"Shoulder. Really no more than a graze. I told Chief not to worry, but I knew he would anyway. I can still help."

"Let me be the judge of that. My medical bag is in the trunk. I'll get it and at least clean and bandage it until we can get you to the hospital."

Crouching, Michael moved to the back of his car and retrieved his bag. Law-enforcement vehicles from the sheriff's department flooded the street, their flashing lights illuminating the darkness. Usually the sight of them brought comfort to Michael that everything would be all right. Not now. What if Wilson decided to shoot his way out, using one or all of the females as a barrier? Or what if Wilson had already killed them? Or…

The gauze package slipped from his numb fingers. *Please, Lord, bring them through safely.*

The wall phone rang. Wilson glared at it and didn't make a move to pick it up.

The strobe of the red lights seeped through the small cracks in the blinds. "You should answer it. See what their deal is." Kyra's fingers dug into the wood of the chair to keep herself from flying at the officer and getting herself shot. She'd been involved in hostage situations before. Remaining calm was important.

"Shut up. I know what they'll say."

The ringing stopped. Positioned by the blinds, Wilson relaxed slightly.

Then the phone pealed again.

The lethal look he gave it should have blown it to smithereens. His rigid stance and knuckle-white clasp on the gun shouted his jittery disposition, which could short-circuit with the slightest provocation. A dangerous time for hostages. Kyra kept her gaze trained on Wilson for any sign she could use to her advantage.

Silence finally reigned—for a moment before Gabe's deep voice boomed over a loudspeaker. "Wilson, this isn't the young man I've gotten to know the past five years. Son, let the ladies go and we can work something out. We can make a deal in exchange for your cooperation."

"You all have no idea who you're up against," Wilson mumbled as though Gabe were standing next to him. "He's a cold-blooded killer who'll think nothing of murdering anyone in his way."

"Who are you talking about?"

Wilson blinked, surprise washing over his face. "No one."

"At least let Amy, Laurie and Ellen go. You can keep me as a hostage. You know how much Gabe cares for me. He won't want anything to happen to me."

Wilson peered toward the dining room, the corner of his mouth jerking. "I'm supposed to kill you all."

"If you do, you are dead for sure. They'll storm this place at the sound of the first gunshot."

"I'm dead anyway if I don't do what he wants."

"There's always a chance the other way. If you have something good to offer, the Witness Security Program has a first-rate reputation for keeping its people safe. Let me talk to Gabe. Work something out for you."

He bit into his lower lip, his eyes penetratingly intense. "I'll trade the girls and Ellen for Gabe."

"Can I get up and use the phone?" She glanced the few feet to the desk where it sat.

"Slowly. I'll kill you if you try anything." The fierce tone behind his words earlier had lost its bluster.

Kyra followed his directions, and when she dialed Gabe's cell, her mentor picked up on the first ring. "Wilson will trade Amy, Laurie and Ellen for you. He wants to talk a deal." She wouldn't blame Gabe if he declined, but he and Wilson had been close. She hoped when confronted with the man who took him under his wing that Wilson would fold and give himself up.

"Have him send out Amy and Laurie, then I'll approach the house and he can let Ellen go at the same time I go inside."

"I'll tell him."

"Is everyone all right?"

"Yes, scared but fine. Is everyone okay out there?"

"Connors was hit in the shoulder, but Michael is patching him up."

Relief fluttered through her. *Michael is safe.* She hung up and faced Wilson, who had advanced within a couple of feet of her. "He agrees to exchange himself."

After she explained Gabe's conditions, Wilson directed her to go into the dining room. "Uncuff them." When Amy and Laurie were freed, he continued. "Take them to the front door and let them out. Remember, I still have the gun and can shoot you or your aunt."

Although she didn't think he would now that he'd made up his mind to listen to Gabe, she wouldn't take a chance with the others' lives by trying to be heroic. She knew how fast a hostage situation could turn with one wrong move. After the girls left, Kyra untied her aunt and escorted her to the entrance, waiting until Gabe was on the porch before opening the door and letting Aunt Ellen leave. The two exchanged a brief smile and traded places. The police chief entered the foyer, his expression calm as though he faced down a gun every day.

"Wilson, I've been on the phone with the county prosecutor. If you can lead us to the man behind these killings, he can reduce your sentence."

"Not good enough. I would die in prison."

"What do you have to offer for immunity?"

"Something big. But I'm not coming in until I get full immunity from prosecution and protection. The information I have is well worth it."

Gabe studied his fellow officer for a long moment. "I need to make some calls."

Wilson tossed his head in the direction of the kitchen. "The phone is in there."

Gabe went into the room first, then Kyra and finally Wilson with his gun pointed at her the whole time. She concentrated on Gabe, ignoring the weapon not far from her, and started praying for a peaceful resolution.

Ten minutes later, after adamant bargaining on his part, Gabe replaced the receiver in its cradle and said, "Done under the condition your information is everything you say it will be."

"It will be. Once I'm in a safe place, I'll tell you all I know."

Gabe held out his hand for Wilson's gun. Several

heartbeats later, the officer finally put the weapon in the police chief's palm. The second he did, Gabe passed it to Kyra, took out his handcuffs and secured his prisoner, then removed the two guns from Wilson's waistband.

Kyra didn't fully breathe until the bracelets were locked around Wilson's wrists behind his back. The tight band around her chest eased for the first time in an hour and oxygen poured into her lungs, filling them deeply.

All she wanted to do was see Michael and put her arms around him. She had imagined him injured or dead several times in the past hour. She never wanted to go through that again. He meant more to her than she'd realized.

Kyra hung back to let Gabe take Wilson out first. As the screen door banged closed, she came into the foyer, the police chief still on the porch with Wilson slightly to his left and a foot in front.

Suddenly the muffled pop of a gun with a suppressor filled the quiet. The young officer stopped, wavered, then collapsed, tumbling down the stairs. Gabe dived to the side behind the railing and large bushes. Several police below the porch scattered. Kyra instantly lunged toward the kitchen entrance as another bullet ripped through the screen.

THIRTEEN

Kyra's right shoulder slammed into the kitchen floor as the bullet flew into the house. She heard its impact—probably into the wall in the foyer. With pain radiating down her arm, she rolled over and pushed to her feet, drawing the Glock she'd gotten back.

The realization that someone had shot Wilson reinforced the high stakes in this case. Something big was going down—more than the murder of two teenage boys.

She hunkered down by the kitchen entrance into the foyer and saw the bullet hole in the wall on the left side of the foyer. Not a straight shot into the house. Was the shooter near the Pattersons' house? In the swamp? Had he been shooting at her? Or Gabe?

The sound of gunshots reeled through the air. She hated not knowing what was going on. She moved to the bay window and stooped low before parting the blinds an inch and scanning the scene outside. Deputies ran toward the swamp at the end of the block, shooting into the thick vegetation.

She crept to the other side of the window to get a different angle on the yard. Where was Michael? Aunt Ellen? Amy? Laurie? Were they hit?

Gabe eased up as the officers plunged into the swamp. The sheriff approached Wilson on the ground. Gabe descended the steps and knelt by his officer, who was down, and checked his pulse at the side of his neck.

Michael rose from behind his car and started for Wilson.

"No, Michael, it isn't safe." Her words came out hoarse, her throat closing as emotions flooded her. She couldn't lose him. So many people had been hurt.

She jumped to her feet and raced for the front door. Outside on the porch, she shouted, "Get back. The shooter may still be out there."

Gabe looked up. "She's right. Wilson's dead anyway."

With his medical bag in his grasp, Michael stopped in his tracks, his expression evolving from surprise to rage as he took in her disheveled appearance. "You're hurt." He strode toward her.

She held up her hand. "I'm fine. Get back."

He ignored her and closed the space between them, charging up the steps. "What did he do to you?" Fury rolled through his voice.

"Nothing. I'm fine." She'd never seen Michael so angry.

"The right side of your face is swollen and red. That's not nothing. It's not safe for you to be out here, either." He took her arm and tugged her toward the front door.

Kyra winced and pulled back, rubbing her shoulder.

"What else is wrong?"

"I fell on my shoulder. It hurts."

"Let me check you out."

"No, I'm all right. I've been hurt worst than this. I want to check on Aunt Ellen and the girls."

"They're fine. They're safe in the sheriff's car and the minute the shooting started the deputy with them drove off."

Kyra entered the house. Exhaustion weighed her legs down as she made her way into the kitchen. She shuddered with weariness and sank down onto a chair. The sudden quiet sent a tremor through her. Was it over? Had they captured the other shooter?

Michael stood at the counter and watched the coffee drip down into the carafe. Mindlessly staring at the plop, plop of the dark brew as it fell. Kyra could have been killed last night because of him. She was involved because of him.

The memory of how she looked when she'd finally gone to bed a few hours ago haunted him.

She would have a black eye; it had already started turning. Her cheek was bruised and swollen. Along with her shoulder. Thankfully, the MRI at the hospital had shown it wasn't anything more serious with the shoulder than sore, tender muscles.

Those injuries weren't that serious, but the fact she was hurt at all bothered him. This had been her vacation, and instead he had placed her in danger a number of times. He couldn't deal with anything happening to her as it did with Sarah.

"You couldn't sleep, either."

Kyra's sweet voice floated to him. Slowly he turned toward her, leaning back against the counter and gripping it on either side of him. "Since the man got away from the deputies last night in the swamp, it's hard not to think about him being out there somewhere. Too much going around and around in my brain."

"Me, too. Especially the possibilities of what the killer is planning." Kyra walked across the room and stopped a foot from him.

He wanted to take her in his arms and never let her go. He wanted to kiss her senseless. His fingers dug into the edge of the countertop. "If we all hadn't been totally exhausted, we should have hashed it out after coming back from the hospital."

"I didn't need to go."

"I'm glad you humored me. I feel bad enough

with what happened to you without wondering if you needed more medical attention."

"At least Laurie got to see her mother and make sure she was all right."

"Gabe is taking Amy's sketch back to Cherie this morning to see if she can add anything to the drawing but both girls think it's pretty accurate."

"I know the killer's picture is important, but I'm concerned about the plans that the girls saw in the duffel bag. We need to concentrate on those and figure out what's going on. If Friday is the deadline, we have one day to come up with answers."

"We don't have to do anything. Let the police figure it out." He clasped her hands, wishing he could deny the bond between them. "You need to rest, take care of yourself."

"While something big might be going down that I could help stop? No, I can't walk away from this. This killer made it personal when he sent Wilson after me." She squeezed his hands, then tugged hers free and pulled a mug from the cabinet to fill with coffee. "I'm going to need tons of this."

Michael poured some for himself and strode to the bay window. He parted the blinds and peered out at the deputy standing guard on the porch. There was another one on the back deck. "It isn't over. We're still in danger."

"Until the killer is caught, yes." Kyra came to his side. "I wouldn't be surprised if Gabe is here soon.

I doubt he's gotten any sleep, either. He looked beat last night."

"It's hard discovering one of your officers has been helping a killer."

"When it's a decent hour, I'm calling a contact I know at the FBI in Washington. We've worked together. I keep thinking about Amy saying the man slipped back and forth between English and Spanish. I know we talked about Preston's cousin being involved in a gang in Miami. I know many people in Miami—this area of Florida—speak both languages, but this killer being here doesn't have anything to do with a gang. From what Gabe could find out, Tyler was here to see his family. We need to ID the killer. I know the state is being brought in, possibly the Feds, but I want to talk to my friend. Maybe this killer isn't from the United States. Why was he hiding out in the Everglades? What is happening on Friday? From what Amy said there was a lot of money in that bag. Why is the man hanging around? Why didn't he leave at the first sign of trouble? Could he be a hit man?"

Michael held up his hand. "Whoa. My mind is on overload. Is this the way you were when you were working as a police detective?"

"I found in my work it was important to ask the right questions if you wanted to discover what was going on."

He cocked a grin. "I imagine you've covered it somewhere in all those you asked."

"It's hard to turn off once I get going."

"I wish I'd never gotten you involved in the first place."

Her forehead wrinkled. "Why?"

He caressed the uninjured side of her face. "You were hurt because you helped me."

She gripped his hand. "Don't you blame yourself for what happened. Like I said, I've had worse happen to me."

"Do you think I like hearing that?"

"Listen, Michael Hunt. I can take care of myself. I've been doing it for years. I don't need a protector."

"Do you need anyone?" The question came out unbidden, but he realized it had been in the back of his mind for a while. Kyra was so capable, as though it were her against the world. He cared about her, and she didn't need someone to care about her.

"What do you mean?"

Michael turned away from the bay window and put several feet between them. Her scent of vanilla was playing havoc with his senses. He couldn't think straight with her so near. "Just that. You're so together. You can handle yourself in tough situations. You were hurt and you didn't even want me to check you out. You told me on more than one occasion you could take care of yourself. I get that now. You don't need anyone."

"No person can go totally alone."

"But isn't that what you've been doing?"

She opened her mouth to say something, but instead of speaking, she snapped it closed, pivoted and strode through the dining room to the living area.

He followed her, leaning against one of the posts that separated the great room from the dining room. "When I was a teenager, you were this girl I couldn't get out of my mind. Then we went our separate ways. I fell in love and thought I would have a life with Sarah. Then it was taken away from me. My world was rocked. My faith was tested. Even my conviction I should be a doctor. I was slowly piecing both back together, and then I see you again. From the first moment I haven't been able to get you out of my mind. But I've just figured out it isn't a two-way street."

He paused, wishing she would deny it—tell him she loved him. That nothing else mattered. But she remained silent, holding her mug between her hands, staring down at her drink.

"I can accept that. Once this is over, we go our separate ways. Because what I need and want from a woman is one hundred percent. I don't think you can give it. You hold part of yourself back."

Finally she lifted her gaze to his. Anger hardened her eyes. "I do? What about you? You are so afraid of losing another loved one that you can't give that hundred percent you want from me. You—"

A knock at the front door interrupted their conversation. Kyra glanced toward the foyer, then headed for it, putting her mug on the desk on her way out of the room.

Michael started to tell her to be careful and not open the door without checking first. He swallowed those words because Kyra wouldn't do something like that. She was cautious in everything, including her emotions, and she still thought of herself as their bodyguard.

The sound of Gabe's voice drifted from the entry hall. A minute later Kyra and the police chief came into the room. Gabe looked tired, with bags under his eyes. Until right now he had never appeared his age of fifty-six. Every year was etched on his face as he stood next to Kyra.

"I couldn't sleep. I figured y'all couldn't, either. We need to figure out why the killer is here. Most people would have fled the area after murdering two young men. This guy is hanging around for a reason. What?"

"It has to do with the plans Amy and Laurie saw in the bag." Kyra picked up her mug and sipped at her coffee.

"What I saw didn't look like much."

Michael pushed off the post. "That's because Amy and Laurie had just started with the plans when everything happened last night."

"While we're waiting for them to get up, let's go over what we have so far. Do you want any coffee, Gabe?" Kyra headed toward the kitchen.

"Yes." The police chief sank into a lounge chair, his movements stiff and slow.

"Is everything okay?" Michael asked, taking a place on the couch across from Gabe.

"No, my body isn't cooperating with my wants. I want to be able to run like I'm twenty. I want to be able to pull all-nighters and still be alert to do my job the next day. I don't think I'm going gracefully into old age. I don't know what I'm going to do about retiring with Wilson gone."

"You'll find someone. Despite what has happened lately, this is a nice town to live in." Kyra handed Gabe his mug and took the other chair.

"Before we get started, we never had a chance to talk about what went down yesterday. Why didn't you tell me about Amy and Laurie contacting you two?" Gabe's probing gaze swung between Kyra and Michael. "I get it about being worried about a corrupt cop. Amy made that clear last night when I talked with her after everything was over, but Kyra, you know me. How could you think I was that officer?"

Pain flitted into her eyes. "I—I…" She swallowed hard.

"It was me." Michael sat forward, his elbows on his thighs. "I made her promise she wouldn't because I couldn't take any chances with my sister's life. She agreed but made it clear to me you weren't the corrupt cop."

Gabe stared at him for a long time. "I'll say this and then it will be done. I don't believe in letting problems and anger stew for days because it doesn't solve anything. I find it just makes things worse. We could have worked as a team to figure out who the cop was that was being paid off. I thought my years of duty would have made it clear the type of person I am."

Michael held his look. "I take full responsibility for the decision. I hope you can understand I had to protect my sister at all costs. I'm sorry if you're upset by what we did. It was never meant as an offense against you but a necessary caution to keep my sister safe."

"Gabe, I knew it wasn't you, but when I give my word, I don't break it."

The police chief lifted his mug and sipped his coffee then put it on the small table next to the chair. "No one has ever accused me of being a touchy-feely kind of guy, but I had to tell you how I felt. Now, let's get down to the business at hand. What is this killer here for?"

Watching as Kyra and Gabe started listing what was known about the man still out there, Michael lounged back and listened. He loved Kyra, but her life was so different from his. After losing Sarah, he realized he couldn't go through that kind of pain again and Kyra thrived on danger. She took risks with her life. It was a good thing they lived hundreds of miles apart because it would never work between them. She could have died last night at Wilson's hand. He needed to shut down how he felt about her before his heart was ripped in two again.

Later that morning Kyra shifted in the chair at the kitchen table, feeling every bit of the hardness of the seat she'd been sitting in for hours. Amy and Laurie were taking a break, the sound of their voices coming from the great room, indicating they were still arguing over details of the plans. Neither had gotten a good long look.

Gabe hung up from talking on his cell. "They ID'd the man. He's called the Black Mamba. No one knows his real name or where he's from. He's an international hit man hired by terrorist groups. The description they had was sketchy, but the black snake tattoo is what nailed it for the Feds. That's the Black Mamba's trademark."

"Any potential targets?" Kyra rose and stretched her cramped muscles.

"The FBI are looking into several targets. The

vice president is coming to Tampa tomorrow for a speech. There's a symposium on terrorism on St. Cloud Island starting Friday with some world leaders attending and there's a conference for oil companies meeting in Marco Island. Any of the three could be a possible target, not to mention someplace like Disney World."

Michael whistled. "In other words, anywhere in Florida could be a potential place for a statement if a terrorist group funded this man."

"Yup. So any help we can give them will be appreciated. An FBI team should be in Flamingo Cay shortly."

"I'm thinking Amy and Laurie have the right idea. We need a break." Michael stood, rolled his head and began pacing.

"I'm meeting with the sheriff in a few minutes at the station to coordinate our end before the FBI show up. I'll be back in an hour, and we can pick up where we left off." Gabe labored to his feet. "I'll bring lunch back. Don't want Ellen to have to worry about it."

After he left, Kyra released the laugh she'd been holding. "I think he's figured out she can't cook and is being as diplomatic as he can."

"Smart man."

"You've been pretty quiet this morning."

"What's there to say? This is your area of expertise. You and Gabe have it handled. I'm not a detective and will be glad when I can get back to what I do best. I've learned one thing. I want to continue being a doctor. It's what I was called to do. Like any job, there are things I wish I didn't have to deal with, but I can't picture doing anything else."

She gestured toward her face. "You do a good job. One I'm grateful for."

His neutral expression evolved into a scowl. "I had to take you kicking and screaming to get an MRI on your shoulder."

"I wasn't that bad."

"You're not a good patient."

"I don't like having something wrong with me."

"Because you might have to depend on another?"

"Is that what's bothering you? For years I worked with a partner, so I know how to play nice with others. I even learned to share." Her muscles still tight, Kyra twisted from side to side.

"What?"

"Opinions, theories on a case, recipes. Whatever needed to be shared."

"How about yourself?"

"What's going on, Michael? Ever since we got up this morning, you've been distancing yourself from me. Are you ready to share yourself? Do you still blame yourself for what happened to Sarah? Have you forgiven yourself for living while she didn't?"

With each question she asked, he backed away a few inches.

"You've become important to me, but I think you're still wrestling with your past. You keep throwing up roadblocks between us. If and when I ever commit myself to a man, I want one hundred percent from him, just as you do from a woman. You aren't ready to do that, are you?"

"Weren't you the one who said you didn't think marriage was for you?"

"Is that what we're talking about?"

He kneaded the cords of his neck. "Yes. No. What we've been going through this past week has been intense, unreal, not normal—at least not for me."

"Believe me, I don't normally run from a killer—not even when I was a detective."

"I've developed feelings for you, but are they really real?"

"Ah, feelings? What kind? Hate? Like?"

He closed the space quickly between them. "Love."

"But you can't see how that could be real because Sarah has only been gone for a year?"

"Exactly."

"You walked away from the accident. She didn't. So do you have a right to go on and be happy?"

"She'd be alive if I hadn't insisted on going. She didn't want to. I worked two shifts at the hospital.

If I hadn't been so tired, I should have been able to prevent the wreck somehow."

She curled her hands into fists to still the urge to cradle his face and kiss him until he realized it was all right to go on living. But this wasn't the time to tell him she'd fallen for him—quickly and hard. She'd always been drawn to him, but since he was Ginny's kid brother she'd tamped down her feelings. Now she couldn't, but he wasn't ready. "God has other plans in store for you. It wasn't your time."

"That's easy to say, but it doesn't erase my guilt in Sarah's death."

"And that's the problem between us. I've decided to leave as soon as this is wrapped up."

"How about your vacation?"

"I can't stay." Kyra met his intense look with one of her own. She loved him, but Sarah stood between them.

"I remember something," Amy charged into the kitchen and made a beeline for the table where the plans were spread out. "I'm not sure what they mean, but there were three of them on the drawings I saw." Michael's sister scribbled something on the paper.

Laurie came up beside her and pointed to another place. "And one here."

"That's right. There were four of them."

Kyra strode to the table. "What?" She stared at

the paper with four X's on it in four totally different areas. "If we knew what building this is, it would be easier, but from my time on the bomb squad, this looks like good places to plant bombs to bring a building down. Of course, that would depend on the size and type of bomb."

"We didn't unroll the plans all the way. Laurie and I are pretty sure there was another wing to this building."

"Okay. A center building with two wings. Let's pull up on the internet views of the location where the symposium, conference and the vice president's speech are taking place."

"We don't know if the building is one story or three or ten."

"If he's planning to blow up a building, taking out the first floor could bring it all down if done right." Kyra lifted the laptop lid and connected to the web.

Early Friday morning, blue sky, with not a cloud in it, stretched as far as Kyra could see. She turned away from the bay window that afforded her a view of Pelican Lane and the front yard where a deputy was still camped out, guarding them. They had passed on all their information to the FBI and state police. Trying to figure out where the killer would strike had been a good way to keep them all occupied. Now, however, they were in the tenth hour of waiting.

"I'm gonna scream if we have to stay inside much longer." Amy stomped into the kitchen, went to the refrigerator and got a can of soda out. "When are we gonna hear anything? I feel like a prisoner."

"Gabe promised to call as soon as he heard anything."

"What if we are wrong? If it isn't the oil companies' conference? We aren't that far from Miami or Key West or Orlando."

"Your drawing best matches the hotel where the oil companies are holding their meeting."

"But the meeting on terrorism makes more sense or the vice president's speech. Didn't Gabe say the Black Mamba worked for terrorist groups?"

Kyra kneaded the back of her neck, tension locking her muscles. "I thought so, too, but the plans don't match."

Her eyes full of uncertainty, Amy folded her arms across her chest. "What if I'm wrong? What if I cause people to die?"

"It won't be your fault, Amy," Michael said from the doorway. "We're doing everything we can to prevent a tragedy. We didn't hire the assassin. The information you and Laurie have given the police has been invaluable. But ultimately this is in the hands of the Lord. All we can do is pray."

"I have been."

"Then you're doing what you can." Michael hugged his sister, his look capturing Kyra's. "Waiting is never easy, but we should hear soon."

Amy sighed.

Kyra shifted her gaze to Amy. "The FBI has set a trap for the Black Mamba. If all goes well, they will catch a world-renowned assassin and stop a tragedy."

The doorbell chimed. Amy gasped. Michael whirled around while Kyra hurried to answer the door.

Gabe beamed from ear to ear. "The FBI trapped the Black Mamba in an evacuated wing where the meeting between the oil companies was taking place. He managed to escape, but he didn't get far. The seaplane he was on crashed into the ocean. He's dead."

Michael stepped out onto his back deck as dawn on Saturday pushed aside night. Another sleepless one. Because he couldn't get Kyra out of his mind. He felt like a teenage boy all over again with a crush on her.

He folded his length into a chair that faced the sea. He inhaled the salty tang that laced the air. The breeze stirred the palm fronds in the trees along the edge of the backyard. A bird trilled in a nearby crepe myrtle. The serenity should have been a balm after all the danger and intensity of the past week. But it didn't soothe his soul.

His life was in a holding pattern. Not moving backward or forward. Just going around and around in circles. He'd come to Flamingo Cay to straighten out his life and had thrown himself into his work, giving himself no time to figure out what to do. Then Kyra had come along and challenged him to give the Lord another chance. To turn his problems over to Him. To trust the plans God had for him. To forgive himself for living while Sarah didn't.

He opened the palm of his hand to reveal the key to Kyra's house, the one he'd forgotten to return when he and Amy had returned home yesterday. She was leaving later this morning. He could take it to her or wait and give it back to Ellen. He didn't have to see Kyra again.

But he wanted to.

Needed to.

He loved her and no amount of excuses on why a relationship wouldn't work between them would change that. She'd told him he needed to deal with his guilt over Sarah. He'd convinced himself that Kyra lived a dangerous life that would eventually take it. He didn't want to be around to mourn her as he had Sarah. Cut his losses. That would be the best thing for him.

But it wasn't.

So how did he forgive himself for living while Sarah died? He was driving the car. He'd insisted they go away for the weekend because he had wanted to ask Sarah to marry him in a special place.

"You can't sleep, either?" Amy said from the doorway.

"No. What's keeping you up?"

"Laurie and her mother."

"Cherie is going to be all right. She's awake and the doctors feel she will have a full recovery."

"She wouldn't have been in the hospital if it weren't for me."

"Why? Because you dropped your phone and the Black Mamba found it and traced your location? Cherie said he'd known about you from a surveillance camera he always sets up wherever he goes. It wasn't your fault." That was the second time in less than twenty-four hours he had said that to his sister. *What are You trying to tell me, Lord?*

"Yes, it was. I'm the one who got us turned around in the Everglades. I agreed with the guys about exploring the cabin when they said they wanted to. Laurie wanted to leave and try and find our way home. I'm to blame for everything."

"Did you pull the trigger and shoot Preston and Tyler?"

She shook her head.

"Did you beat up Laurie's mother?"

"No, but—"

"Did you want those things to happen to them? If you could, would you have stopped them from happening?"

"Yes."

Michael leaned forward in his chair, his own words reaching deep into his heart to heal a wound. "Forgive yourself. Learn from the experience. You got lost in the Glades. That's happened to a lot of people before. You wanted to explore a new place. That doesn't surprise me. New things have always held wonder for you. You can't change the past, but you can make something of the present and your future."

"I've never been so scared. When Laurie and me were hiding from that man, we kept talking about all the things we might never get to do."

"You've been given a second chance. All those things are waiting for you."

Tears in her eyes, Amy came over to him and threw her arms around him, kissing his cheeks. "I love you, big brother."

"Hey, you ain't too bad yourself."

She clasped his hands and tugged on him. "Come on. Let's go get breakfast at the Watering Hole. Pancakes with strawberries and whipped cream."

"Sounds delicious."

"I'll go see if Laurie is awake."

Michael rose as his sister hurried into the house. He peered four houses down and spotted the hibiscus hedge along this side of Kyra's family home. Was she up yet? Probably not but he would go see her after he got back from breakfast with his sister and Laurie.

Because God had given him a second chance, too.

Kyra walked across the sand to where the waves broke onto the shore. Five days ago not much earlier than today she'd come out to the beach to begin her vacation and now it was over. She would fly out later today from Miami. Home to Dallas and back to her normal life. A day earlier than planned.

Last night the house had been so empty with Michael and the girls gone. Even Aunt Ellen had gone out to dinner with Gabe in Naples, leaving her alone although they had asked her to come. She hadn't wanted to intrude on their first official date. Then this morning he was at the house bright and early to take Aunt Ellen for target practice.

The warm water flowed over her flip-flops. At least the innocent people of the world were rid of the Black Mamba. Too bad there were others ready to take the assassin's place.

She turned to stroll back toward the house to finish packing. She needed to be on the road in a few hours, but she had wanted to come out here and at least spend some time on the beach enjoying what she had looked forward to for months. Maybe when Ginny returned to the United States and Flamingo Cay, she could come back for another vacation—preferably a calm, safe one. But for now she couldn't stay with Michael so close.

She trudged up the steps to the deck and rinsed off her feet before entering the back door. This was where she and Michael had said their good-byes the night before with the room full of people. After Gabe arrived yesterday, she and Michael had no time to be alone. She'd preferred it that way—less painful. She prayed one day he'd find some peace and forgive himself for surviving the car crash.

As she made her way across the oblong great room, a tingling along her nape caused her to slow her pace. She couldn't shake the sensation eyes were boring into her. She glanced down at her waist where her holster had often been this past week. Nothing.

Every fiber of her being screamed she wasn't alone. Everyone connected to this case was dead. Was there a fourth person they hadn't known about?

She kept placing one foot in front of the other while her mind frantically tried to come up with a way to get out of the situation alive. The tingling sensation spread down her length as though a target were being drawn on her back.

"Turn around slowly," a deep, gravelly voice said.

Kyra did as she was told and came face-to-face with the Black Mamba.

Michael mounted the stairs to Kyra's back deck and crossed it to knock on the door. His raised hand paused in midair. Through the glass he glimpsed the back of a tall, medium-built man with a gun pointed at Kyra. On his arm at his side was a tattoo of a black snake. The Black Mamba was alive?

Michael stepped away from the door and retrieved his cell from his pocket. While striding toward the garage door, he called Gabe to report the assassin in Kyra's house.

"You stay away. We can be there in five minutes."

Michael clicked off and unlocked the garage's side door. Five minutes might be too long. It only took a second to pull a trigger.

As he sneaked into Kyra's kitchen, he heard the man called the Black Mamba say, "No one damages my reputation and gets away with it. I'm going to kill you, then take care of your doctor friend and those two girls."

Michael scanned the room for any kind of weapon he could use against the man. He pulled open the drawer of the desk where he'd seen Ellen put her gun once. Empty. Then his gaze lit upon the cast-iron skillet on the stove. He grabbed it and peeked around the door frame into the dining room. He didn't see the Black Mamba but his voice came to Michael as though he still stood in the same place a couple of feet from the opening into the great room from the foyer.

If he could surprise the man, he could knock him out without a shot fired. Michael eased forward. *Lord, I can't do this without You.*

Flattening himself against the wall, Michael peered around the corner into the room. The Black Mamba's back was still to him. Kyra saw him as he crept toward the killer but somehow managed not to give anything away.

Her focus returned to the assassin, totally directed at him. "You won't get away. If I turn up dead, the authorities will know you're alive."

He laughed. "That's okay. They might figure it out when they don't find my body with the debris from the airplane crash. I have places I can disappear to and hide. I don't usually kill unless I'm paid for it, but I'm making an exception here." He raised his gun arm higher.

Michael hoisted the skillet and swung it toward the man's head. The sound of the impact with his skull reverberated through the room. The weapon dropped to the tile while the man teetered for a few seconds, then sank to the floor.

Kyra scrambled forward and scooped up the gun. As she straightened, her look riveted to Michael.

Silence dominated for a brief moment. Then suddenly Kyra flew into his arms and crushed herself against him, raining kisses all over his face.

Later when all the confusion died down and the army of people with the Black Mamba in tow had left Pelican Lane, Michael took Kyra's hand and pulled her across her deck, down the steps and out onto the beach, the rays of the sun warming them as they strolled along the sandy shoreline.

"I'm so glad you chose that moment to return my key or..."

"Don't say it. God's given us a second chance. I know we have some hurdles to overcome to make a relationship work for us, but I want to try. I love you. Have ever since I first saw you when I was eight years old."

She chuckled. "No, you didn't. You tossed a water balloon at me and drenched me. I don't call that love."

"To an eight-year-old boy, it's our way of showing our interest in the opposite sex."

"I think you need to work on your technique."

He stopped in the sand and turned her toward

him, winding his arms around her and planting a kiss on her mouth—long, deep, soul-healing.

"Is that better?"

"Mmm. It's getting there, but I think you'll have to practice some more—say, a lifetime."

"Where? Here or Dallas?"

"Details to be worked out later. The only important one is we love each other." She pulled his head down for another kiss.

EPILOGUE

Kyra scanned the sea of people gathered in the recreational hall at her church in Dallas. Her friends and family were all here to celebrate her wedding day. Until she'd reacquainted herself with Michael a year ago, she hadn't thought she would ever wear a white gown and walk down the aisle toward her husband to be. Only an hour ago she'd proved herself wrong.

"What are you smiling about, Mrs. Hunt?"

She shifted toward Michael, the feeling they could face anything together washing over her. "You. All these people here today. Even a few from Flamingo Cay."

"I'm going to miss that place."

"You're still okay with moving here and setting up a practice?" The past year until Amy was ready to go away to college had been hard with her and Michael flying back and forth between Dallas and Flamingo Cay. But they had forged a deeper relationship due to their separation through the year. She had learned to cherish each second with him.

"Yes, especially since they found another doctor to replace me. No more emergency medicine for me. Family practice suits me just fine." He leaned forward and brushed his mouth across hers.

"That's no way to kiss your new wife." Gabe grinned, a twinkle in his eye. "Come on. You can do better than that."

Surrounded by family—Ginny, Amy, her sister, Amanda, and Aunt Ellen—as well as friends— fellow Dallas police officers, her employees at Guardians, Inc., Ken and his wife—Kyra wasn't going to let them down. Amidst applause and cheering, she curled her arm around Michael and dragged him closer.

"I certainly don't want to disappoint them," Kyra whispered against his mouth right before she deepened the kiss and surrendered anew her heart to her husband.

* * * * *

Dear Reader,

This is the last book in the Guardians, Inc. series. I have enjoyed trying to put myself in the mind-set of a female hired to protect a person. Although Kyra is tough and knows how to take care of herself, she has a fear of snakes that started when she was a child and had a terrifying experience with one. Even the strongest people have weaknesses.

I love hearing from readers. You can contact me at margaretdaley@gmail.com or at P.O. Box 2074 Tulsa, OK 74101. You can learn more about my books at www.margaretdaley.com. I have a quarterly newsletter that you can sign up for on my website or you can enter my monthly drawings by signing my guest book on the website.

Best wishes,

Margaret Daley

QUESTIONS FOR DISCUSSION

1. Kyra couldn't wait to go on vacation and finally relax and rest. Do you find life gets so busy you hardly enjoy what is happening? What are some things you can do to pause and enjoy the moment?

2. What is your favorite scene? Why?

3. Fear can make people do things they wouldn't normally do. Amy didn't know whom to trust. She ran because she was frightened and put herself and her friend in danger. Have you ever let fear rule your life? What did you do to overcome the fear?

4. Kyra has seen enough marriages in her lifetime that have ended badly that she doesn't want to have anything to do with that kind of commitment. What makes a marriage strong? What kind of advice would you give her about marriage?

5. Who is your favorite character? Why?

6. What lengths would you go to in order to protect a loved one?

7. Kyra didn't tell Gabe about Amy and Laurie being found. Gabe was upset with her and felt a little betrayed, but in the end forgave her for keeping that from him. Have you ever had something like that happen to you with a friend? How did you resolve the situation?

8. Who did you think was the corrupt law-enforcement officer? Why?

9. Michael felt guilty about Sarah dying in the wreck. Guilt can do a lot of harm to a person. How can guilt be displayed in a person?

10. Michael felt in over his head dealing with raising Amy, a rebellious seventeen-year-old. What advice would you give him as far as Amy was concerned?

11. Michael was questioning whether he should be a doctor. He'd tried to save Sarah's life at the wreck, but she died. He had been working long hours and now it seemed like as if efforts were for nothing. Have you ever felt burned out? How do you rejuvenate yourself? How do you avoid becoming burned out in the first place?

12. Kyra had to face a childhood fear of snakes in the story. She didn't want to go into the Everglades but she did because Michael needed her.

Do you have a fear of something like Kyra did? Have you had to face a fear like that and had to overcome it? How did you do it?

13. Michael's faith was tested when he lost Sarah. He didn't think the Lord was listening to him. Have you ever thought that? What did you do to work through that? How do you know that the Lord is listening even though He doesn't always answer your prayers the way you want?

14. What do you think of female bodyguards? Would you trust one to guard you? Why or why not?

15. As a police officer Kyra saw the dark side of life. She had to quit being a police officer or lose herself. How can people who serve to protect us keep from having the dark side of life pull them down?

LARGER-PRINT BOOKS!

**GET 2 FREE
LARGER-PRINT NOVELS
PLUS 2 FREE
MYSTERY GIFTS**

Love Inspired
SUSPENSE
RIVETING INSPIRATIONAL ROMANCE

Larger-print novels are now available...

LARGER-PRINT BOOKS!

GET 2 FREE
LARGER-PRINT NOVELS
PLUS 2 FREE
MYSTERY GIFTS

Love Inspired

Larger-print novels are now available...